The Feast

Compiled by SIMON WINDER

✗ ✗ ✗

PENGUIN BOOKS

In memory of JDSW

PENGUIN BOOKS

Published by the Penguin Group
Penguin Books Ltd, 27 Wrights Lane, London w8 5tz, England
Penguin Putnam Inc., 375 Hudson Street, New York, New York 10014, USA
Penguin Books Australia Ltd, Ringwood, Victoria, Australia
Penguin Books Canada Ltd, 10 Alcorn Avenue, Toronto, Ontario, Canada m4v 3b2
Penguin Books (NZ) Ltd, Private Bag 102902, NSMC, Auckland, New Zealand

Penguin Books Ltd, Registered Offices: Harmondsworth, Middlesex, England

First published in Penguin Books 1998
1 3 5 7 9 10 8 6 4 2

Set in 10/12.5 pt PostScript Adobe Minion
Typeset by Rowland Phototypesetting Ltd, Bury St Edmunds, Suffolk
Printed in England by Clays Ltd, St Ives plc

Contents

Publisher's Note

To write some complex apologia for a book on eating and drinking would be a fruitless exercise. There is *no* wider justification for *The Feast* than that each extract chosen is either appealing or peculiar or exotic. Some of the material is well known (*A Christmas Carol*, *The Owl and the Pussy-Cat*) and some very obscure; some mouthwatering and some less so. Great efforts have been made to avoid *The Feast* turning into a mere catalogue of vacuous heartiness ('. . . and we rounded things off with a goodly chunk of Stilton cheese') and this is achieved, I hope, by scattering sufficient uneasy or emetic material throughout the text to keep the browser off balance.

While drawing from the vast range of Penguin's list, *The Feast* had to be compiled on the basis that only English-language texts could be considered. Given that the topic is eating and drinking this was clearly a self-mutilating decision. The riches of the Anglo-American *literary* tradition are readily balanced by the happy laughter provoked in much of the world by the leaden Anglo-American *culinary* tradition. Balzac on the wine and food of the Loire, Mishima on dinner etiquette or Herodotus on the giant-tailed sheep of Arabia would have immeasurably enriched *The Feast* but any attempt at coherence would have collapsed under the sheer grandeur and range of the Penguin Classics' list. As it is, readers will notice a heavy reliance on English translations of Horace and Martial (drawn from the remarkable *Poets in Translation* series) which extends the range of food and drink references without breaking the boundaries completely.

Inevitably important elements have been missed out. As with the other compilations *Night Thoughts* and *Sea Longing*, *The Feast* makes not authoritative claims. It aims simply to give its readers a chance to bump into a some remarkable poetry or prose, perhaps not otherwise encountered. While otherwise entirely made up of extracts and short poems, *The Feast* includes two longer whole items – Saki's *The Byzantine Omelette* (because it would be pointless and crude to rip a piece off such a perfect, short, short story) and Rosetti's *Goblin Market* (because it is such a delirious, marvellous poem that any opportunity to reproduce it whole must be jumped at).

This collection is dedicated to the memory of a great creator and celebrator of feasts who in spirit will *always* be at the head of the table.

Simon Winder
August 1998

The Feast

The fat boy rose, opened his eyes, swallowed the huge piece of pie he had been in the act of masticating when he last fell asleep, and slowly obeyed his master's orders.

Charles Dickens *The Pickwick Papers*

They had scraped up fresh river fish, and stewed them with white wine and aubergines; also a rare local bird which combined the tender flavour of partridge with the solid bulk of the turkey; they had roasted it and stuffed it with bananas, almonds and red peppers; also a baby gazelle which they had seethed with truffles in its mother's milk; also a dish of feathery Arab pastry and a heap of unusual fruits. Mr Baldwin sighed wistfully, 'Well,' he said, 'I suppose it will not hurt us to rough it for once.'

Evelyn Waugh *Scoop*

O madness! to think use of strongest wines
And strongest drinks our chief support of health . . .

John Milton *Samson Agonistes*

Dinner at Castle Dracula

The light and warmth and the Count's courteous welcome seemed to have dissipated all my doubts and fears. Having then reached my normal state, I discovered that I was half-famished with hunger; so making a hasty toilet, I went into the other room.

I found supper already laid out. My host, who stood on one side of the great fireplace, leaning against the stone-work, made a graceful wave of his hand to the table, and said:

'I pray you, be seated and sup how you please. You will, I trust, excuse me that I do not join you; but I have dined already, and I do not sup.'

BRAM STOKER
from *Dracula*

'Now al is done; bring home the bride againe'

Now al is done; bring home the bride againe,
Bring home the triumph of our victory,
Bring home with you the glory of her gaine,
With joyance bring her and with jollity.
Never had man more joyfull day then this,
Whom heaven would heape with blis.
Make feast therefore now all this live long day,
This day for ever to me holy is,
Poure out the wine without restraint or stay,
Poure not by cups, but by the belly full,
Poure out to all that wull,

And sprinkle all the postes and wals with wine,
That they may sweat, and drunken be withall.
Crowne ye God Bacchus with a coronall,
And Hymen also crowne with wreathes of vine,
And let the Graces daunce unto the rest;
For they can doo it best:
The whiles the maydens doe theyr carroll sing,
To which the woods shal answer and theyr eccho ring.

EDMUND SPENSER
from *Epithalamion*

To the Immortal Memory of the Halibut on which I Dined this Day

Where hast thou floated, in what seas pursued
Thy pastime? When wast thou an egg new-spawned,
Lost in the immensity of ocean's waste?
Roar as they might, the overbearing winds
That rocked the deep, thy cradle, thou wast safe,
And in thy minikin and embryo state,
Attached to the firm leaf of some salt weed,
Didst outlive tempests, such as wrung and racked
The joints of many a stout and gallant bark,
And whelmed them in the unexplored abyss.
Indebted to no magnet and no chart,
Nor under guidance of the polar fire,
Thou wast a voyager on many coasts,
Grazing at large in meadows submarine,
Where flat Batavia just emerging peeps
Above the brine, where Caledonia's rocks
Beat back the surge, and where Hibernia shoots
Her wondrous causeway far into the main.

Wherever thou hast fed, thou little thought'st,
And I not more, that I should feed on thee.
Peace therefore and good health and much good fish
To him who sent thee, and success, as oft
As it descends into the billowy gulph,
To the same drag that caught thee. Fare thee well.

Thy lot thy brethren of the slimy fin
Would envy, could they know that thou wast doomed
To feed a bard and to be praised in verse.

WILLIAM COWPER

Appetite

... He who distinguishes the true savor of his food can never
be a glutton; he who does not cannot be otherwise. A puritan
may go to his brown-bread crust with as gross an appetite as
ever an alderman to his turtle. Not that food which entereth
into the mouth defileth a man, but the appetite with which it
is eaten. It is neither the quality nor the quantity, but the
devotion to sensual savors; when that which is eaten is not a
viand to sustain our animal, or inspire our spiritual life, but
food for the worms that possess us. If the hunter has a taste for
mud-turtles, muskrats, and other such savage tid-bits, the fine
lady indulges a taste for jelly made of a calf's foot, or for sardines
from over the sea, and they are even. He goes to the mill-pond,
she to her preserve-pot. The wonder is how they, how you and
I, can live this slimy beastly life, eating and drinking.

HENRY DAVID THOREAU
from Walden

The Prioress

Ther was also a Nonne, a PRIORESSE,
That of hir smylyng was ful symple and coy;
Hire gretteste ooth was but by Seinte Loy;
And she was cleped madame Eglentyne.
Ful weel she soong the service dyvyne,
Entuned in hir nose ful semely;
And Frenssh she spak ful faire and fetisly,
After the scole of Stratford atte Bowe,
For Frenssh of Parys was to hire unknowe.
At mete wel ytaught was she with alle;
She leet no morsel from hir lippes falle,
Ne wette hir fyngres in hir sauce depe;
Wel koude she carie a morsel and wel kepe
That no drope ne fille upon hire brest.
In curteisie was set ful muchel hir lest.
Hir over-lippe wyped she so clene
That in hir coppe ther was no ferthyng sene
Of grece, whan she dronken hadde hir draughte.
Ful semely after hir mete she raughte.
And sikerly she was of greet desport,
And ful pleasaunt, and amyable of port,
And peyned hire to countrefete cheere
Of court, and to been estatlich of manere,
And to ben holden digne of reverence.
But for to speken of hire conscience,
She was so charitable and so pitous
She wolde wepe, if that she saugh a mous
Kaught in a trappe, if it were deed or bledde.
Of smale houndes hadde she that she fedde

With rosted flessh, or milk and wastel-breed.
But soore wepte she if oon of hem were deed,
Or if men smoot it with a yerde smerte;
And al was conscience and tendre herte.

GEOFFREY CHAUCER
from *The General Prologue*

Dinner with the Grand Vizier's Lady

She entertain'd me with all kind of Civillity till Dinner came
in, which was serv'd one Dish at a time, to a vast Number, all
finely dress'd after their manner, which I do not think so bad
as you have perhaps heard it represented. I am a very good
Judge of their eating, having liv'd 3 weeks in the house of an
Effendi at Belgrade who gave us very magnificent dinners dress'd
by his own Cooks, which the first week pleas'd me extremely,
but I own I then begun to grow weary of it and desir'd my
own Cook might add a dish or 2 after our manner, but I
attribute this to Custom. I am very much enclin'd to beleive
an Indian that had never tasted of either would prefer their
Cookery to ours. Their Sauces are very high, all the roast
very much done. They use a great deal of rich Spice. The Soop
is serv'd for the last dish, and they have at least as great Variety
of ragoûts as we have. I was very sorry I could not eat of as
many as the good Lady would have had me, who was very
earnest in serving me of every thing. The Treat concluded with
Coffee and perfume which is a high mark of respect. 2 slaves
kneeling cens'd my Hands Cloaths, and handkerchief. After this
Ceremony she commanded her Slaves to play and dance, which
they did with their Guitars in their hands, and she excus'd to

me their want of skill, saying she took no care to accomplish
them in that art. I return'd her thanks and soon after took my
Leave.

LADY MARY WORTLEY MONTAGU

'He lands us on a grassy stage'

He lands us on a grassy stage,
Safe from the storms, and prelate's rage.
He gave us this eternal spring,
Which here enamels everything,
And sends the fowl to us in care,
On daily visits through the air.
He hangs in shades the orange bright,
Like golden lamps in a green night,
And does in the pom'granates close
Jewels more rich than Ormus shows.
He makes the figs our mouths to meet,
And throws the melons at our feet,
But apples plants of such a price,
No tree could ever bear them twice.

ANDREW MARVELL
from 'Bermudas'

The Owl and the Pussy-Cat

I

The Owl and the Pussy-Cat went to sea
   In a beautiful pea-green boat,
They took some honey, and plenty of money,
   Wrapped up in a five-pound note.
The Owl looked up to the stars above,
   And sang to a small guitar,
'O lovely Pussy! O Pussy, my love,
   'What a beautiful Pussy you are,
      'You are,
      'You are!
   'What a beautiful Pussy you are!'

II

Pussy said to the Owl, 'You elegant fowl!
   'How charmingly sweet you sing!
'O let us be married! too long we have tarried:
   'But what shall we do for a ring?'
They sailed away for a year and a day,
   To the land where the Bong-tree grows,
And there in a wood a Piggy-wig stood,
   With a ring at the end of his nose,
      His nose,
      His nose,
   With a ring at the end of his nose.

III

'Dear Pig, are you willing to sell for one shilling
   'Your ring?' Said the Piggy, 'I will.'
So they took it away, and were married next day
   By the Turkey who lives on the hill.

They dined on mince, and slices of quince,
Which they ate with a runcible spoon;
And hand in hand, on the edge of the sand,
They danced by the light of the moon,
The moon,
The moon,
They danced by the light of the moon.

EDWARD LEAR

Pub [1942]

The glasses are raised, the voices drift into laughter,
The clock hands have stopped, the beer in the hands of the
    soldiers
Is blond, the faces are calm and the fingers can feel
The wet touch of glasses, the glasses print rings on the table,
The smoke rings curl and go up and dissolve near the ceiling,
       This moment exists and is real.

What is reality? Do not ask that. At this moment
Look at the butterfly eyes of the girls, watch the barmaid's
Precision in pouring a Scotch, and remember this day,
This day at this moment you were no longer an island,
People were friendly, the clock in the hands of the soldiers
       For this moment had nothing to say.

And nothing to say and the glasses are raised, we are happy
Drinking through time, and a world that is gentle and helpless
Survives in the pub and goes up in the smoke of our breath,
The regulars doze in the corner, the talkers are fluent;
Look now in the faces of those you love and remember
       That you are not thinking of death.

But thinking of death as the lights go out and the glasses
Are lowered, the people go out, and the evening
Goes out, ah, goes out like a light and leaves you alone,
As the heart goes out, the door opens out into darkness,
The foot takes a step, and the moment, the moment of falling
      Is here, you go down like a stone.

Are you able to meet the disaster, able to meet the
Cold air of the street and the touch of corruption, the rotting
Fingers that murder your own in the grip of love?
Can you bear to find hateful the faces you once thought were
    lovely,
Can you bear to find comfort alone in the evil and stunted,
      Can you bear to abandon the dove?

The houses are shut and the people go home, we are left in
Our islands of pain, the clocks start to move and the powerful
To act, there is nothing now, nothing at all
To be done: for the trouble is real: and the verdict is final
Against us. The clocks go round faster and faster. And fast as
    confetti
      The days are beginning to fall.

JULIAN SYMONS

Of the Street-sellers of Cakes, Tarts, &c.

These men and boys – for there are very few women or girls in
the trade – constitute a somewhat numerous class. They are
computed (including Jews) at 150 at the least, all regular hands,
with an addition, perhaps, of 15 or 20, who seek to earn a
few pence on a Sunday, but have some other, though poorly
remunerative, employment on the week-days. The cake and
tart-sellers in the streets have been, for the most part, mechanics

or servants; a fifth of the body, however, have been brought up to this or to some other street-calling.

The cake-men carry their goods on a tray slung round their shoulders when they are offering their delicacies for sale, and on their heads when not engaged in the effort to do business. They are to be found in the vicinity of all public places. Their goods are generally arranged in pairs on the trays; in bad weather they are covered with a green cloth.

None of the street-vendors make the articles they sell: indeed, the diversity of those articles renders that impossible. Among the regular articles of this street-sale are 'Coventrys', or three-cornered puffs with jam inside; raspberry biscuits; cinnamon biscuits; 'chonkeys', or a kind of mince-meat baked in crust; Dutch butter-cakes; Jews' butter-cakes; 'bowlas', or round tarts made of sugar, apple, and bread; 'jumbles', or thin crisp cakes made of treacle, butter, and flour; and jams, or open tarts with a little preserve in the centre.

All these things are made for the street-sellers by about a dozen Jew pastry-cooks, the most of whom reside about Whitechapel. They confine themselves to the trade, and make every description. On a fine holiday morning their shops, or rather bake-houses, are filled with customers, as they supply the small shops as well as the street-sellers of London. Each article is made to be sold at a halfpenny, and the allowance by the wholesale pastry-cook is such as to enable his customers to realise a profit of 4d. in 1s.; thus he charges 4d. a dozen for the several articles. Within the last seven years there has been, I am assured, a great improvement in the composition of these cakes, &c. This is attributable to the Jews having introduced superior dainties, and, of course, rendered it necessary for the others to vie with them; the articles vended by these Jews (of whom there are from 20 to 40 in the streets) are still pronounced, by many connoisseurs in street-pastry, as the best. Some sell penny dainties also, but not to a twentieth part of the halfpenny trade.

One of the wholesale pastry-cooks takes 40l. a week. These wholesale men, who sometimes credit the street-people, buy ten, fifteen, or twenty sacks of flour at a time whenever a cheap bargain offers. They purchase as largely in Irish butter, which they have bought at 3d. or 2½d. the pound. They buy also 'scrapings', or what remains in the butter-firkins when emptied by the butter-sellers in the shops. 'Good scrapings' are used for the best cakes; the jam they make themselves. To commence the wholesale business requires a capital of 60ol. To commence the street-selling requires a capital of only 10s.; and this includes the cost of a tray, about 1s. 9d.; a cloth 1s.; and a leathern strap, with buckle, to go round the neck, 6d.; while the rest is for stock, with a shilling or two as a reserve. All the street-sellers insist upon the impossibility of any general baker making cakes as cheap as those they vend. 'It's impossible, sir,' said one man to me, 'it's a trade by itself; nobody else can touch it. They was miserable little things seven years ago.'

HENRY MAYHEW
from *London Labour and the London Poor*

To Autumn

I

Season of mists and mellow fruitfulness,
  Close bosom-friend of the maturing sun,
Conspiring with him how to load and bless
  With fruit the vines that round the thatch-eves run;
To bend with apples the mossed cottage-trees,
  And fill all fruit with ripeness to the core;
    To swell the gourd, and plump the hazel shells
  With a sweet kernel; to set budding more,

And still more, later flowers for the bees,
Until they think warm days will never cease,
　　For Summer has o'er-brimmed their clammy cells.

II

Who hath not seen thee oft amid thy store?
　　Sometimes whoever seeks abroad may find
Thee sitting careless on a granary floor,
　　Thy hair soft-lifted by the winnowing wind;
Or on a half-reaped furrow sound asleep,
　　Drowsed with the fume of poppies, while thy hook
　　　　Spares the next swath and all its twinèd flowers;
And sometimes like a gleaner thou dost keep
　　Steady thy laden head across a brook;
　　Or by a cider-press, with patient look,
　　　　Thou watchest the last oozings hours by hours.

III

Where are the songs of Spring? Ay, where are they?
　　Think not of them, thou hast thy music too –
While barrèd clouds bloom the soft-dying day,
　　And touch the stubble-plains with rosy hue:
Then in a wailful choir the small gnats mourn
　　Among the river sallows, borne aloft
　　　　Or sinking as the light wind lives or dies;
And full-grown lambs loud bleat from hilly bourn;
　　Hedge-crickets sing; and now with treble soft
　　The red-breast whistles from a garden-croft;
　　　　And gathering swallows twitter in the skies.

JOHN KEATS

On Attwater's Atoll

They sat down to an island dinner, remarkable for its variety and excellence; turtle soup and steak, fish, fowls, a sucking pig, a cocoanut salad, and sprouting cocoanut roasted for dessert. Not a tin had been opened; and save for the oil and vinegar in the salad, and some green spears of onion which Attwater cultivated and plucked with his own hand, not even the condiments were European. Sherry, hock, and claret succeeded each other, and the *Farallone* champagne brought up the rear with the dessert.

It was plain that, like so many of the extremely religious in the days before teetotalism, Attwater had a dash of the epicure. For such characters it is softening to eat well; doubly so to have designed and had prepared an excellent meal for others; and the manners of their host were agreeably mollified in consequence. A cat of huge growth sat on his shoulders purring, and occasionally, with a deft pew, capturing a morsel in the air. To a cat he might be likened himself, as he lolled at the head of his table, dealing out attentions and innuendoes, and using the velvet and the claw indifferently. And both Huish and the captain fell progressively under the charm of his hospitable freedom.

Over the third guest, the incidents of the dinner may be said to have passed for long unheeded. Herrick accepted all that was offered him, ate and drank without tasting, and heard without comprehension. His mind was singly occupied in contemplating the horror of the circumstances in which he sat. What Attwater knew, what the captain designed, from which side treachery was to be first expected, these were the ground of his thoughts.

ROBERT LOUIS STEVENSON
from *The Ebb-Tide*

Pie Fillings

'Weal pie,' said Mr Weller, soliloquising, as he arranged the eatables on the grass. 'Wery good thing is a weal pie, when you know the lady as made it, and is quite sure it an't kittens; and arter all though, where's the odds, when they're so like weal that the wery piemen themselves don't know the difference?'

'Don't they, Sam?' said Mr Pickwick.

'Not they, Sir,' replied Mr Weller, touching his hat. 'I lodged in the same house vith a pieman once, Sir, and a wery nice man he was – reg'lar clever chap, too – make pies out o' anything, he could. "What a number o' cats you keep, Mr Brooks," says I, when I'd got intimate with him. "Ah," says he, "I do – a good many," says he. "You must be wery fond o' cats," says I. "Other people is," says he, a winkin' at me; "they an't in season till the winter though," says he. "Not in season!" says I. "No," says he, "fruits is in, cats is out." "Why, what do you mean?" says I. "Mean?" says he. "That I'll never be a party to the combination o' the butchers, to keep up the prices o' meat," says he. "Mr Weller," says he, squeezing my hand wery hard, and vispering in my ear – "don't mention this here agin, but it's the seasonin' as does it. They're all made o' them noble animals," says he, a pointin' to a wery nice little tabby kitten, "and I seasons 'em for beef-steak, weal, or kidney, 'cordin' to the demand; and more than that," says he, "I can make a weal a beef-steak, or a beef-steak a kidney, or any one on 'em a mutton, at a minute's notice, just as the market changes, and appetites wary!"'

'He must have been a very ingenious young man, that, Sam,' said Mr Pickwick, with a slight shudder.

'Just was, Sir,' replied Mr Weller, continuing his occupation of emptying the basket, 'and the pies was beautiful. Tongue; well that's a wery good thing, when it an't a woman's. Bread –

knuckle o' ham, reg'lar picter – cold beef in slices, wery good. What's in them stone jars, young touch-and-go?'

'Beer in this one,' replied the boy, taking from his shoulder a couple of large stone bottles, fastened together by a leathern strap – 'cold punch in t'other.'

'And a wery good notion of a lunch it is, take it altogether,' said Mr Weller, surveying his arrangement of the repast with great satisfaction. 'Now, gen'l'men, "fall on," as the English said to the French when they fixed bagginets.'

It needed no second invitation to induce the party to yield full justice to the meal; and as little pressing did it require, to induce Mr Weller, the long gamekeeper, and the two boys, to station themselves on the grass at a little distance, and do good execution upon a decent proportion of the viands. An old oak tree afforded a pleasant shelter to the group, and a rich prospect of arable and meadow land, intersected with luxuriant hedges, and richly ornamented with wood, lay spread out below them.

'This is delightful – thoroughly delightful!' said Mr Pickwick, the skin of whose expressive countenance, was rapidly peeling off, with exposure to the sun.

'So it is – so it is, old fellow,' replied Wardle. 'Come; a glass of punch.'

'With great pleasure,' said Mr Pickwick; and the satisfaction of his countenance after drinking it, bore testimony to the sincerity of the reply.

'Good,' said Mr Pickwick, smacking his lips. 'Very good. I'll take another. Cool; very cool. Come, gentlemen,' continued Mr Pickwick, still retaining his hold upon the jar, 'a toast. Our friends at Dingley Dell.'

The toast was drunk with loud acclamations.

'I'll tell you what I shall do, to get up my shooting again,' said Mr Winkle, who was eating bread and ham with a pocket-knife. 'I'll put a stuffed partridge on the top of a post, and practise at it, beginning at a short distance, and lengthening it by degrees. I understand it's capital practice.'

'I know a gen'l'man, Sir,' said Mr Weller, 'as did that, and begun at two yards; but he never tried it on agin; for he blowed the bird right clean away at the first fire, and nobody ever seed a feather on him arterwards.'

'Sam,' said Mr Pickwick.

'Sir,' replied Mr Weller.

'Have the goodness to reserve your anecdotes, 'till they are called for.'

'Cert'nly, Sir.'

CHARLES DICKENS
from *The Pickwick Papers*

'What? Quarrel in your drink, my friends?'

What? Quarrel in your drink, my friends? ye' abuse
   Glasses, and Wine, made for a better use.
'Tis a Dutch trick; Fie, let your brawling cease,
   And from your Wine and Olives learn both mirth and
      peace.

Your swords drawn in a Tavern, whilest the hand
   That holds them shakes, and he that fights cann't stand,
Sheath 'um for shame, embrace, kiss, so away,
   Sit down, and ply the business of the day.
But I'le not drink, unless T.S. declares
   Who is his Mistress, and whose wounds he wears,
Whence comes the glance, from what sweet-killing-Eye,
   That sinks his Hope so low, and mounts his Muse so high!
Wilt thou not tell? Drawer, what's to pay?
   If you're reserv'd I'le neither drink nor stay:

Or let me go, or out w'it; she must be
   Worth naming, sure; whose Fate it was to conquer thee:
Speak softly – She! forbid it Heaven above!
   Unhappy youth! unhappy in thy love;
Oh how I pity thy Eternal pain!
   Thou never can'st get loose, thou never canst obtain;
Lets talk no more of love, my friends, lets drink again.

'DR P.'

At the Cavour

Wine, the red coils, the flaring gas,
   Bring out a brighter tone in cheeks
That learn at home before the glass
   The flush that eloquently speaks.

The blue-grey smoke of cigarettes
   Curls from the lessening ends that glow;
The men are thinking of the bets,
   The women of the debts, they owe.

Then their eyes meet, and in their eyes
   The accustomed smile comes up to call,
A look half miserably wise,
   Half heedlessly ironical.

ARTHUR SYMONS

Dinner in Vienna

I have already had the Honour of being invited to Dinner by several of the first people of Quality, and I must do them the Justice to say the good taste and Magnificence of their Tables very well answers to that of their Furniture. I have been more than once entertain'd with 50 dishes of meat, all serv'd in silver and well dress'd, the desert proportionable, serv'd in the finest china; but the variety and richnesse of their wines is what appears the most surprizing. The constant way is to lay a list of their names upon the plates of the Guests along with the napkins, and I have counted several times to the number of 18 different sorts, all exquisite in their kinds. I was yesterday at Count Schonbourn's, the vice chancellor's Garden, where I was invited to Dinner, and I must own that I never saw a place so perfectly delightfull as the Fauxbourgs of Vienna. It is very large and almost wholly compos'd of delicious Palaces; and if the Emperor found it proper to permit the Gates of the Town to be laid open that the Fauxbourgs might be joyn'd to it, he would have one of the largest and best built Citys of Europe. Count Schonbourne's Villa is one of the most magnificent, the Furniture all rich brocards, so well fancy'd and fited up, nothing can look more Gay and Splendid, not to speak of a Gallery full of raritys of Coral, mother of Pearl, etc., and through out the whole House a profusion of Gilding, Carving, fine paintings, the most beautifull Porcelane, statues of Alablaster and Ivory, and vast Orange and Lemon Trees in Gilt Pots. The Dinner was perfectly fine and well-order'd and made still more agreable by the Good humour of the Count.

LADY MARY WORTLEY MONTAGU

'O DAVID, highest in the list'

O DAVID, highest in the list
Of worthies, on God's ways insist,
    The genuine word repeat:
Vain are the documents of men,
And vain the flourish of the pen
    That keeps the fool's conceit.

Praise above all – for praise prevails;
Heap up the measure, load the scales,
    And good to goodness add:
The generous soul her saviour aids,
But peevish obloquy degrades;
    The Lord is great and glad.

For ADORATION all the ranks
Of angels yield eternal thanks,
    And DAVID in the midst;
With God's good poor which, last and least
In man's esteem, thou to thy feast,
    O blessed bridegroom, bidst.

For ADORATION seasons change,
And order, truth, and beauty range,
    Adjust, attract, and fill:
The grass the polyanthus cheques;
And polish'd porphyry reflects
    By the descending rill.

Rich almonds colour to the prime
For ADORATION; tendrils climb,
    And fruit-trees pledge their gems;

And Ivis, with her gorgeous vest,
Builds for her eggs her cunning nest,
   And bell-flowers bow their stems.

With vinous syrup cedars sprout;
From rocks pure honey gushing out
   For ADORATION springs:
All scenes of painting crowd the map
Of nature; to the mermaid's pap
   The scalèd infant clings.

The spotted ounce and playsome cubs
Run rustling 'mongst the flow'ring shrubs,
   And lizards feed the moss;
For ADORATION beasts embark,
While waves upholding halcyon's ark
   No longer roar and toss.

While Israel sits beneath his fig,
With coral root and amber sprig
   The wean'd advent'rer sports;
Where to the palm the jasmin cleaves,
For ADORATION 'mongst the leaves
   The gale his peace reports.

CHRISTOPHER SMART
from *A Song to David*

At the Wagon and Horses

'Now, then, all together, boys,' some one would shout, and the
company would revert to old favourites. Of these, one was 'The
Barleymow'. Trolled out in chorus, the first verse went:

Oh, when we drink out of our noggins, my boys,
  We'll drink to the barleymow.
We'll drink to the barleymow, my boys,
  We'll drink to the barleymow.
So knock your pint on the settle's back;
  Fill again, in again, Hannah Brown,
We'll drink to the barleymow, my boys,
  We'll drink now the barley's mown.

So they went on, increasing the measure in each stanza, from noggins to half-pints, pints, quarters, gallons, barrels, hogsheads, brooks, ponds, rivers, seas, and oceans. That song could be made to last a whole evening, or it could be dropped as soon as they got tired of it.

Another favourite for singing in chorus was 'King Arthur', which was also a favourite for outdoor singing and was often heard to the accompaniment of the jingling of harness and cracking of whips as the teams went afield. It was also sung by solitary wayfarers to keep up their spirits on dark nights. It ran:

When King Arthur first did reign
  He ru-led like a king;
He bought three sacks of barley meal
  To make a plum pud-ding.

The pudding it was made
  And duly stuffed with plums,
And lumps of suet put in it
  As big as my two thumbs.

The king and queen sat down to it
  And all the lords beside;
And what they couldn't eat that night
  The queen next morning fried.

Every time Laura heard this sung she saw the queen, a gold crown on her head, her train over her arm, and her sleeves rolled up, holding the frying-pan over the fire. Of course, a queen *would* have fried pudding for breakfast: ordinary common people seldom had any left over to fry.

FLORA THOMPSON
from *Lark Rise*

The Bowl of Rack Punch

The two couples were perfectly happy then in their box: where the most delightful and intimate conversation took place. Jos was in his glory, ordering about the waiters with great majesty. He made the salad; and uncorked the Champagne; and carved the chicken; and ate and drank the greater part of the refreshments on the tables. Finally, he insisted upon having a bowl of rack punch; everybody had rack punch at Vauxhall. 'Waiter, rack punch.'

That bowl of rack punch was the cause of all this history. And why not a bowl of rack punch as well as any other cause? Was not a bowl of prussic acid the cause of Fair Rosamond's retiring from the world? Was not a bowl of wine the cause of the demise of Alexander the Great, or, at least, does not Dr Lemprière say so? – so did this bowl of rack punch influence the fates of all the principal characters in this 'Novel without a Hero', which we are now relating. It influenced their life, although most of them did not taste a drop of it.

The young ladies did not drink it; Osborne did not like it; and the consequence was that Jos, that fat *gourmand*, drank up the whole contents of the bowl; and the consequence of his drinking up the whole contents of the bowl was, a liveliness which at first was astonishing, and then became almost painful; for he talked and laughed so loud as to bring scores of listeners round the box, much to the confusion of the innocent party within it; and, volunteering to sing a song (which he did in that maudlin high key peculiar to gentlemen in an inebriated state), he almost drew away the audience who were gathered round the musicians in the gilt scollop-shell, and received from his hearers a great deal of applause.

'Brayvo, Fat un!' said one; 'Angcore, Daniel Lambert!' said another; 'What a figure for the tight-rope!' exclaimed another wag, to the inexpressible alarm of the ladies, and the great anger of Mr Osborne.

'For Heaven's sake, Jos, let us get up and go,' cried that gentleman, and the young women rose.

'Stop, my dearest, diddle-diddle-darling,' shouted Jos, now as bold as a lion, and clasping Miss Rebecca round the waist. Rebecca started, but she could not get away her hand. The laughter outside redoubled. Jos continued to drink, to make love, and to sing; and, winking and waving his glass gracefully to his audience, challenged all or any to come in and take a share of his punch.

WILLIAM MAKEPEACE THACKERAY
from *Vanity Fair*

The Poetry of a Root Crop

Underneath their eider-robe
Russet swede and golden globe,
Feathered carrot, burrowing deep,
Steadfast wait in charmèd sleep;
Treasure-houses wherein lie,
Locked by angels' alchemy,
Milk and hair, and blood, and bone,
Children of the barren stone;

Children of the flaming Air,
With his blue eye keen and bare,
Spirit-peopled smiling down
On frozen field and toiling town –
Toiling town that will not heed
God His voice for rage and greed;
Frozen fields that surpliced lie,
Gazing patient at the sky;
Like some marble carven nun,
With folded hands when work is done,
Who mute upon her tomb doth pray,
Till the resurrection day.

CHARLES KINGSLEY

The Digestive System

See, how the human animal is fed,
How nourishment is wrought, and how conveyed:
The mouth, with proper faculties endued,
First entertains, and then divides, the food;
Two adverse rows of teeth the meat prepare,
On which the glands fermenting juice confer;
Nature has various tender muscles placed,
By which the artful gullet is embraced;
Some the long funnel's curious mouth extend,
Through which ingested meats with ease descend;
Other confederate pairs for Nature's use
Contract the fibres, and the twitch produce,
Which gently pushes on the grateful food
To the wide stomach, by its hollow road;
That this long road may unobstructed go,
As it descends, it bores the midriff through;

The large receiver for concoction made
Behold amidst the warmest bowels laid;
The spleen to this, and to the adverse side
The glowing liver's comfort is applied;
Beneath, the pancreas has its proper seat,
To cheer its neighbour, and augment its heat;
More to assist it for its destined use,
This ample bag is stored with active juice,
Which can with ease subdue, with ease unbind,
Admitted meats of every different kind;
This powerful ferment, mingling with the parts,
The leavened mass to milky chyle converts;
The stomach's fibres this concocted food,
By their contraction's gentle force, exclude,
Which by the mouth on the right side descends
Through the wide pass, which from that mouth depends;
In its progression soon the laboured chyle
Receives the confluent rills of bitter bile,
Which by the liver severed from the blood,
And striving through the gall-pipe, here unload
Their yellow streams, more to refine the flood;
The complicated glands, in various ranks
Disposed along the neighbouring channel's banks,
By constant weeping mix their watery store
With the chyle's current, and dilute it more;
Th'intestine roads, inflicted and inclined,
In various convolutions turn and wind,
That these meanders may the progress stay,
And the descending chyle, by this delay,
May through the milky vessels find its way,
Whose little mouths in the large channel's side
Suck in the flood, and drink the cheering tide.
These numerous veins (such is the curious frame!)
Receive the pure insinuating stream;

But no corrupt or dreggy parts admit,
To form the blood, or feed the limbs unfit;
Th'intestine spiral fibres these protrude,
And from the winding tubes at length exclude.

SIR RICHARD BLACKMORE

The Byzantine Omelette

Sophie Chattel-Monkheim was a Socialist by conviction and a Chattel-Monkheim by marriage. The particular member of that wealthy family whom she had married was rich, even as his relatives counted riches. Sophie had very advanced and decided views as to the distribution of money: it was a pleasing and fortunate circumstance that she also had the money. When she inveighed eloquently against the evils of capitalism at drawing-room meetings and Fabian conferences she was conscious of a comfortable feeling that the system, with all its inequalities and iniquities, would probably last her time. It is one of the consolations of middle-aged reformers that the good they inculcate must live after them if it is to live at all.

On a certain spring evening, somewhere towards the dinner-hour, Sophie sat tranquilly between her mirror and her maid, undergoing the process of having her hair built into an elaborate reflection of the prevailing fashion. She was hedged round with a great peace, the peace of one who has attained a desired end with much effort and perseverance, and who has found it still eminently desirable in its attainment. The Duke of Syria had consented to come beneath her roof as a guest, was even now installed beneath her roof, and would shortly be sitting at her dining-table. As a good Socialist, Sophie disapproved of social distinctions, and derided the idea of a princely caste, but if there were to be these artificial gradations of rank and dignity she was pleased and anxious to have an exalted specimen of an exalted order included in her house-party. She was broad-minded enough to love the sinner while hating the sin – not that she entertained any warm feeling of personal affection for the Duke of Syria, who was a comparative stranger, but still, as Duke of Syria, he was very, very welcome beneath her roof. She could not have explained why, but no one was likely to ask her for an explanation, and most hostesses envied her.

'You must surpass yourself tonight, Richardson,' she said complacently to her maid; 'I must be looking my very best. We must all surpass ourselves.'

The maid said nothing, but from the concentrated look in her eyes and the deft play of her fingers it was evident that she was beset with the ambition to surpass herself.

A knock came at the door, a quiet but peremptory knock, as of some one who would not be denied.

'Go and see who it is,' said Sophie; 'it may be something about the wine.'

Richardson held a hurried conference with an invisible mess-enger at the door; when she returned there was noticeable a curious listlessness in place of her hitherto alert manner.

'What is it?' asked Sophie.

'The household servants have "downed tools", madame,' said Richardson.

'Downed tools!' exclaimed Sophie; 'do you mean to say they've gone on strike?'

'Yes, madame,' said Richardson, adding the information: 'It's Gaspare that the trouble is about.'

'Gaspare?' said Sophie wonderingly; 'the emergency chef! The omelette specialist!'

'Yes, madame. Before he became an omelette specialist he was a valet, and he was one of the strike-breakers in the great strike at Lord Grimford's two years ago. As soon as the household staff here learned that you had engaged him they resolved to "down tools" as a protest. They haven't got any grievance against you personally, but they demand that Gaspare should be immediately dismissed.'

'But,' protested Sophie, 'he is the only man in England who understands how to make a Byzantine omelette. I engaged him specially for the Duke of Syria's visit, and it would be impossible to replace him at short notice. I should have to send to Paris, and the Duke loves Byzantine omelettes. It was the one thing we talked about coming from the station.'

'He was one of the strike-breakers at Lord Grimford's,' reiterated Richardson.

'This is too awful,' said Sophie; 'a strike of servants at a moment like this, with the Duke of Syria staying in the house. Something must be done immediately. Quick, finish my hair and I'll go and see what I can do to bring them round.'

'I can't finish your hair, madame,' said Richardson quietly, but with immense decision. 'I belong to the union and I can't do another half-minute's work till the strike is settled. I'm sorry to be disobliging.'

'But this is inhuman!' exclaimed Sophie tragically; 'I've always been a model mistress and I've refused to employ any but union servants, and this is the result. I can't finish my hair myself; I don't know how to. What am I to do? It's wicked!'

'Wicked is the word,' said Richardson; 'I'm a good Conservative, and I've no patience with this Socialist foolery, asking your pardon. It's tyranny, that's what it is, all along the line, but I've my living to make, same as other people, and I've got to belong to the union. I couldn't touch another hairpin without a strike permit, not if you was to double my wages.'

The door burst open and Catherine Malsom raged into the room.

'Here's a nice affair,' she screamed, 'a strike of household servants without a moment's warning, and I'm left like this! I can't appear in public in this condition.'

After a very hasty scrutiny Sophie assured her that she could not.

'Have they *all* struck?' she asked her maid.

'Not the kitchen staff,' said Richardson, 'they belong to a different union.'

'Dinner at least will be assured,' said Sophie, 'that is something to be thankful for.'

'Dinner!' snorted Catherine, 'what on earth is the good of dinner when none of us will be able to appear at it? Look at your hair – and look at me! or rather, don't.'

'I know it's difficult to manage without a maid; can't your husband be any help to you?' asked Sophie despairingly.

'Henry? He's in worse case than any of us. His man is the only person who really understands that ridiculous new-fangled Turkish bath that he insists on taking with him every-where.'

'Surely he could do without a Turkish bath for one evening,' said Sophie; 'I can't appear without hair, but a Turkish bath is a luxury.'

'My good woman,' said Catherine, speaking with a fearful intensity, 'Henry was *in* the bath when the strike started. *In* it, do you understand? He's there now.'

'Can't he get out?'

'He doesn't know how to. Every time he pulls the lever marked "release" he only releases hot steam. There are two kinds of steam in the bath, "bearable" and "scarcely bearable"; he has released them both. By this time I'm probably a widow.'

'I simply can't send away Gaspare,' wailed Sophie; 'I should never be able to secure another omelette specialist.'

'Any difficulty that I may experience in securing another husband is of course a trifle beneath any one's consideration,' said Catherine bitterly.

Sophie capitulated: 'Go,' she said to Richardson, 'and tell the Strike Committee, or whoever are directing this affair, that

Gaspare is herewith dismissed. And ask Gaspare to see me presently in the library, when I will pay him what is due to him and make what excuses I can; and then fly back and finish my hair.'

Some half an hour later Sophie marshalled her guests in the Grand Salon preparatory to the formal march to the dining-room. Except that Henry Malsom was of the ripe raspberry tint that one sometimes sees at private theatricals representing the human complexion, there was little outward sign among those assembled of the crisis that had just been encountered and surmounted. But the tension had been too stupefying while it lasted not to leave some mental effects behind it. Sophie talked at random to her illustrious guest, and found her eyes straying with increasing frequency towards the great doors through which would presently come the blessed announcement that dinner was served. Now and again she glanced mirror-ward at the reflection of her wonderfully coiffed hair, as an insurance underwriter might gaze thankfully at an overdue vessel that had ridden safely into harbour in the wake of a devastating hurricane. Then the doors opened and the welcome figure of the butler entered the room. But he made no general announcement of a banquet in readiness, and the doors closed behind him; his message was for Sophie alone.

'There is no dinner, madame,' he said gravely; 'the kitchen staff have "downed tools". Gaspare belongs to the Union of Cooks and Kitchen Employés, and as soon as they heard of his summary dismissal at a moment's notice they struck work. They demand his instant reinstatement and an apology to the union. I may add, madame, that they are very firm; I've been obliged even to hand back the dinner rolls that were already on the table.'

After the lapse of eighteen months Sophie Chattel-Monkheim is beginning to go about again among her old haunts and associates, but she still has to be very careful. The doctors will not let her attend anything at all exciting, such as a drawing-room meeting or a Fabian conference; it is doubtful, indeed, whether she wants to.

SAKI

Song

Here's to the maiden of bashful fifteen;
Here's to the widow of fifty;
Here's to the flaunting, extravagant quean,
And here's to the housewife that's thrifty.

CHORUS Let the toast pass,
           Drink to the lass,
I'll warrant she'll prove an excuse for the glass!

Here's to the charmer whose dimples we prize;
Now to the maid who has none, sir!
Here's to the girl with a pair of blue eyes,
And here's to the nymph with but *one*, sir!

CHORUS Let the toast pass, etc.

Here's to the maid with a bosom of snow;
Now to her that's brown as a berry:
Here's to the wife with a face full of woe,
And now to the girl that is merry.

CHORUS Let the toast pass, etc.

For let 'em be clumsy, or let 'em be slim,
Young or ancient, I care not a feather;
So fill a pint bumper quite up to the brim,
And let us e'en toast them together.

CHORUS Let the toast pass, etc.

RICHARD BRINSLEY SHERIDAN
from *The School for Scandal*

The Restaurant Vallet

The Restaurant Vallet, like many of its neighbours, had been originally a clean tranquil little creamery, consisting of a small shop a few feet either way. Then one after another its customers had lost their reserve: they had asked, in addition to their daily glass of milk, for côtes de pré salé and similar massive nourishment, which the decent little business at first supplied with timid protest. But perpetual scenes of unbridled voracity, semesters of compliance with the most brutal appetites of man, gradually brought about a change in its character; it became frankly a place where the most full-blooded palate might be satisfied. As trade grew the small business had burrowed backwards into the ramshackle house: bursting through walls and partitions, flinging down doors, it discovered many dingy rooms in the interior that it hurriedly packed with serried cohorts of eaters. It had driven out terrified families, had hemmed the apoplectic concierge in her 'loge', it had broken out on to the court at the back in shed-like structures: and in the musty bowels of the house it had established a broiling luridly lighted roaring den, inhabited by a fierce band of slatternly savages.

WYNDHAM LEWIS
from *Tarr*

Green Leeks

For it is every Cook's Opinion;
No savoury Dish without an Onion.
And, lest your Kissing should be spoil'd,
Your Onions must be thoroughly boil'd:
          Or else you may spare
          Your Mistress a Share,
The Secret will never be known;
          She cannot discover
          The Breath of a Lover,
But think it as sweet as her own.

JONATHAN SWIFT

The Cook

A Cook they hadde with hem for the nones
To boille the chiknes with the marybones,
And poudre-marchant tart and galyngale.
Wel koude he knowe a draughte of Londoun ale.
He koude rooste, and sethe, and broille, and frye,
Maken mortreux, and wel bake a pye.
But greet harm was it, as it thoughte me,
That on his shyne a mormal hadde he.
For blankmanger, that made he with the beste.

GEOFFREY CHAUCER
from *The General Prologue*

The Tea-Party

There was a table set out under a tree in front of the house, and the March Hare and the Hatter were having tea at it: a Dormouse was sitting between them, fast asleep, and the other two were using it as a cushion, resting their elbows on it, and talking over its head. 'Very uncomfortable for the Dormouse,' thought Alice; 'only as it's asleep, I suppose it doesn't mind.'

The table was a large one, but the three were all crowded together at one corner of it. 'No room! No room!' they cried out when they saw Alice coming. 'There's *plenty* of room!' said Alice indignantly, and she sat down in a large arm-chair at one end of the table.

'Have some wine,' the March Hare said in an encouraging tone.

Alice looked all round the table, but there was nothing on it but tea. 'I don't see any wine,' she remarked.

'There isn't any,' said the March Hare.

'Then it wasn't very civil of you to offer it,' said Alice angrily.

'It wasn't very civil of you to sit down without being invited,' said the March Hare.

'I didn't know it was *your* table,' said Alice: 'it's laid for a great many more than three.'

'Your hair wants cutting,' said the Hatter. He had been looking at Alice for some time with great curiosity, and this was his first speech.

'You should learn not to make personal remarks,' Alice said with some severity: 'it's very rude.'

The Hatter opened his eyes very wide on hearing this; but all he *said* was 'Why is a raven like a writing-desk?'

'Come, we shall have some fun now!' thought Alice. 'I'm glad they've begun asking riddles – I believe I can guess that,' she added aloud.

'Do you mean that you think you can find out the answer to it?' said the March Hare.

'Exactly so,' said Alice.

'Then you should say what you mean,' the March Hare went on.

'I do,' Alice hastily replied; 'at least – at least I mean what I say – that's the same thing, you know.'

'Not the same thing a bit!' said the Hatter. 'Why, you might just as well say that "I see what I eat" is the same thing as "I eat what I see"!'

'You might just as well say,' added the March Hare, 'that "I like what I get" is the same thing as "I get what I like"!'

'You might just as well say,' added the Dormouse, which seemed to be talking in its sleep, 'that "I breathe when I sleep" is the same thing as "I sleep when I breathe"!'

'It *is* the same thing with you,' said the Hatter, and here the conversation dropped, and the party sat silent for a minute, while Alice thought over all she could remember about ravens and writing-desks, which wasn't much.

The Hatter was the first to break the silence. 'What day of the month is it?' he said, turning to Alice: he had taken his watch out of his pocket, and was looking at it uneasily, shaking it every now and then, and holding it to his ear.

Alice considered a little, and then said 'The fourth.'

'Two days wrong!' sighed the Hatter. 'I told you butter wouldn't suit the works!' he added, looking angrily at the March Hare.

'It was the *best* butter,' the March Hare meekly replied.

'Yes, but some crumbs must have got in as well,' the Hatter grumbled: 'you shouldn't have put it in with the bread-knife.'

The March Hare took the watch and looked at it gloomily:

then he dipped it into his cup of tea, and looked at it again: but
he could think of nothing better to say than his first remark, 'It
was the *best* butter, you know.'

LEWIS CARROLL
from *Alice's Adventures in Wonderland*

The Bee and the Pineapple

A bee allured by the perfume
Of a rich pineapple in bloom,
Found it within a frame enclosed,
And licked the glass that interposed.
Blossoms of apricot and peach,
The flowers that blowed within his reach,
Were arrant drugs compared with that
He strove so vainly to get at.
No rose could yield so rare a treat,
Nor jessamine was half so sweet.
The gardener saw this much ado,
(The gardener was the master too)
And thus he said – 'Poor restless bee!
I learn philosophy from thee –
I learn how just it is and wise,
To use what Providence supplies,
To leave fine titles, lordships, graces,
Rich pensions, dignities and places,
Those gifts of a superior kind,
To those for whom they were designed.
I learn that comfort dwells alone
In that which Heaven has made our own,
That fools incur no greater pain
Than pleasure coveted in vain.'

WILLIAM COWPER

The Kitchens at Epsom

Here we are! Let us go into the basement. First into the weighing-house, where the jockeys 'come to scale' after each race. We then inspect the offices for the Clerk of the Course himself; wine-cellars, beer-cellars, larders, sculleries, and kitchens, all as gigantically appointed, and as copiously furnished as if they formed part of an Ogre's Castle. To furnish the refreshment-saloon, the Grand Stand has in store two thousand four hundred tumblers, one thousand two hundred wine-glasses, three thousand plates and dishes, and several of the most elegant vases we have seen out of the Glass Palace, decorated with artificial flowers. An exciting odour of cookery meets us in our descent. Rows of spits are turning rows of joints before blazing walls of fire. Cooks are trussing fowls; confectioners are making jellies; kitchen-maids are plucking pigeons; huge crates of boiled tongues are being garnished on dishes. One hundred and thirty legs of lamb, sixty-five saddles of lamb, and one hundred and thirty shoulders of lamb; in short, a whole flock of sixty-five lambs have to be roasted, and dished, and garnished, by the Derby Day. Twenty rounds of beef, four hundred lobsters, one hundred and fifty tongues, twenty fillets of veal, one hundred sirloins of beef, five hundred spring chickens, three hundred and fifty pigeon-pies; a countless number of quartern loaves, and an incredible quantity of ham have to be cut up into sandwiches; eight hundred eggs have got to be boiled for the pigeon-pies and salads. The forests of lettuces, the acres of cress, and beds of radishes, which will have to be chopped up; the gallons of 'dressing' that will have to be poured out and converted into salads for the insatiable Derby Day, will be best understood by a memorandum from the chief of that department to the *chef-de-cuisine*, which happened, accidentally, to fall under our notice: 'Pray don't forget a large tub and a birch-broom for mixing the salad!'

CHARLES DICKENS
from 'Epsom'

Mrs Duchemin's Breakfast

She was rearranging in a glass bowl some minute flowers that floated on water. They made there, on the breakfast-table, a patch, as it were, of mosaic amongst silver chafing dishes, silver épergnes piled with peaches in pyramids, and great silver rose-bowls filled with roses that drooped to the damask cloth. A congeries of silver largenesses made as if a fortification for the head of the table; two huge silver urns, a great silver kettle on a tripod and a couple of silver vases filled with the extremely tall blue spikes of delphiniums that, spreading out, made as if a fan. The eighteenth-century room was very tall and long; panelled in darkish wood. In the centre of each of four of the panels, facing the light, hung pictures, a mellowed orange in tone, representing mists and the cordage of ships in mists at sunrise. On the bottom of each large gold frame was a tablet bearing the ascription: 'J. M. W. Turner'. The chairs, arranged along the long table that was set for eight people had the delicate, spidery, mahogany backs of Chippendale; on the golden mahogany sideboard that had behind it green silk curtains on a brass-rail were displayed an immense, crumbed ham, more peaches on an épergne, a large meat-pie with a varnished crust, another épergne that supported the large pale globes of grape-fruit, a galantine, a cube of inlaid meats, encased in thick jelly.

FORD MADOX FORD
from *Some Do Not . . .*

The Sultan and the Dervise

The feast was usher'd in – but sumptuous fare
He shunn'd as if some poison mingled there.
For one so long condemn'd to toil and fast,
Methinks he strangely spares the rich repast.
'What ails thee, Dervise? eat – dost thou suppose
This feast a Christian's? or my friends thy foes?
Why dost thou shun the salt? that sacred pledge,
Which, once partaken, blunts the sabre's edge,
Makes even contending tribes in peace unite,
And hated hosts seem brethren to the sight!'

'Salt seasons dainties – and my food is still
The humblest root, my drink the simplest rill;
And my stern vow and order's laws oppose
To break or mingle bread with friends or foes;
It may seem strange – if there be aught to dread,
That peril rests upon my single head;
But for thy sway – nay more – thy Sultan's throne,
I taste nor bread nor banquet – save alone;
Infringed our order's rule, the Prophet's rage
To Mecca's dome might bar my pilgrimage.'
'Well – as thou wilt – ascetic as thou art –
One question answer; then in peace depart.

How many? – Ha! it cannot sure be day?
What star – what sun is bursting on the bay?
It shines a lake of fire! – away – away!
Ho! treachery! my guards! my scimitar!
The galleys feed the flames – and I afar!
Accursed Dervise! – these thy tidings – thou
Some villain spy – seize – cleave him – slay him now!'

Up rose the Dervise with that burst of light,
Nor less his change of form appall'd the sight:
Up rose that Dervise – not in saintly garb,
But like a warrior bounding on his barb,
Dash'd his high cap, and tore his robe away –
Shone his mail'd breast, and flash'd his sabre's ray!

LORD BYRON
from *The Corsair*

Christmas at Chainmail Hall

The party which was assembled on Christmas-day in Chainmail
Hall, comprised all the guests at Crotchet Castle, some of Mr
Chainmail's other neighbours, all his tenants and domestics,
and Captain Fitzchrome. The hall was spacious and lofty; and
with its tall fluted pillars and pointed arches, its windows of
stained glass, its display of arms and banners intermingled with
holly and mistletoe, its blazing cressets and torches, and a
stupendous fire in the centre, on which blocks of pine were
flaming and crackling, had a striking effect on eyes unaccus-
tomed to such a dining-room. The fire was open on all sides, and
the smoke was caught and carried back, under a funnel-formed
canopy, into a hollow central pillar. This fire was the line of
demarcation between gentle and simple, on days of high festival.
Tables extended from it on two sides, to nearly the end of the
hall.

Mrs Chainmail was introduced to the company. Young Crotchet felt some revulsion of feeling at the unexpected sight of
one whom he had forsaken, but not forgotten, in a condition
apparently so much happier than his own. The lady held out
her hand to him with a cordial look of more than forgiveness;
it seemed to say that she had much to thank him for. She was

the picture of a happy bride, *rayonnante de joie et d'amour*.

. . .

The harper at the head of the hall struck up an ancient march, and the dishes were brought in, in grand procession.

The boar's head, garnished with rosemary, with a citron in its mouth, led the van. Then came tureens of plum-porridge; then a series of turkeys, and, in the midst of them, an enormous sausage, which it required two men to carry. Then came geese and capons, tongues and hams, the ancient glory of the Christmas pie, a gigantic plum-pudding, a pyramid of minced pies, and a baron of beef bringing up the rear.

. . .

Ale and wine flowed in abundance. The dinner passed off merrily; the old harper playing all the while the oldest music in his repertory.

THOMAS LOVE PEACOCK
from *Crotchet Castle*

Love (3)

Love bade me welcome: yet my soul drew back,
        Guilty of dust and sin.
But quick-eyed Love, observing me grow slack
        From my first entrance in,
Drew nearer to me, sweetly questioning,
        If I lacked anything.

A guest, I answered, worthy to be here:
        Love said, You shall be he.
I the unkind, ungrateful? Ah my dear,
        I cannot look on thee.
Love took my hand, and smiling did reply,
        Who made the eyes but I?

Truth Lord, but I have marred them: let my shame
    Go where it doth deserve.
And know you not, says Love, who bore the blame?
    My dear, then I will serve.
You must sit down, says Love, and taste my meat:
    So I did sit and eat.

GEORGE HERBERT

The Wassaile

1. Give way, give way ye Gates, and win
An easie blessing to your Bin,
And Basket, by our entring in.

2. May both with manchet stand repleat;
Your Larders too so hung with meat,
That though a thousand, thousand eat;

3. Yet, ere twelve *Moones* shall whirl about
Their silv'rie Spheres, ther's none may doubt,
But more's sent in, then was serv'd out.

4. Next, may your Dairies Prosper so,
As that your pans no Ebbe may know;
But if they do, the more to flow.

5. Like to a solemne sober Stream
Bankt all with Lillies, and the Cream
Of sweetest *Cow-slips* filling Them.

6. Then, may your Plants be prest with Fruit,
Nor Bee, or Hive you have be mute;
But sweetly sounding like a Lute.

7. Next may your Duck and teeming Hen
Both to the Cocks-tread say *Amen*;
And for their two egs render ten.

8. Last, may your Harrows, Shares and Ploughes,
Your Stacks, your Stocks, your sweetest Mowes,
All prosper by your Virgin-vowes.

9. Alas! we blesse, but see none here,
That brings us either Ale or Beere;
In a drie-house all things are neere.

10. Let's leave a longer time to wait,
Where Rust and Cobwebs bind the gate;
And all live here with *needy Fate.*

11. Where Chimneys do for ever weepe,
For want of warmth, and Stomachs keepe
With noise, the servants eyes from sleep.

12. It is in vain to sing, or stay
Our free-feet here; but we'l away:
Yet to the Lares this we'l say,

13. The time will come, when you'l be sad,
And reckon this for fortune bad,
T'ave lost the good ye might have had.

ROBERT HERRICK

In a Bath Teashop

'Let us not speak, for the love we bear one another –
  Let us hold hands and look.'
She, such a very ordinary little woman;
  He, such a thumping crook;
But both, for a moment, little lower than the angels
  In the teashop's ingle-nook.

SIR JOHN BETJEMAN

The Magpie and Stump

This favoured tavern, sacred to the evening orgies of Mr Lowten
and his companions, was what ordinary people would designate
a public-house. That the landlord was a man of a money-making
turn, was sufficiently testified by the fact of a small bulk-head
beneath the tap-room window, in size and shape not unlike a
sedan-chair, being underlet to a mender of shoes: and that he
was a being of a philanthropic mind, was evident from the
protection afforded to a pie-man, who vended his delicacies
without fear of interruption, on the very door-step. In the lower
windows, which were decorated with curtains of a saffron hue,
dangled two or three printed cards, bearing reference to Devon-
shire cyder and Dantzic spruce, while a large black board,
announcing in white letters to an enlightened public, that there
were 500,000 barrels of double stout in the cellars of the establish-
ment, left the mind in a state of not unpleasing doubt and
uncertainty, as to the precise direction in the bowels of the
earth, in which this mighty cavern might be supposed to extend.
When we add, that the weather-beaten sign-board bore the
half-obliterated semblance of a magpie intently eyeing a crooked

streak of brown paint, which the neighbours had been taught from infancy to consider as the 'stump', we have said all that need be said, of the exterior of the edifice.

CHARLES DICKENS
from *The Pickwick Papers*

The Marquis of Granby

The Marquis of Granby, in Mrs Weller's time, was quite a model of a road-side public-house of the better class – just large enough to be convenient, and small enough to the snug. On the opposite side of the road was a large sign-board on a high post, representing the head and shoulders of a gentleman with an apoplectic countenance, in a red coat, with deep blue facings, and a touch of the same over his three-cornered hat, for a sky. Over that again, were a pair of flags; and beneath the last button of his coat were a couple of cannon; and the whole formed an expressive and undoubted likeness of the Marquis of Granby of glorious memory. The bar window displayed a choice collection of geranium plants, and a well-dusted row of spirit phials. The open shutters bore a variety of golden inscriptions, eulogistic of good beds and neat wines; and the choice group of countrymen and hostlers lounging about the stable-door and horse-trough, afforded presumptive proof of the excellent quality of the ale and spirits which were sold within. Sam Weller paused, when he dismounted from the coach, to note all these little indications of a thriving business, with the eye of an experienced traveller; and having done so, stepped in at once, highly satisfied with everything he had observed.

CHARLES DICKENS
from *The Pickwick Papers*

The Great White Horse

In the main street of Ipswich, on the left-hand side of the way, a short distance after you have passed through the open space fronting the Town Hall, stands an inn known far and wide by the appellation of 'The Great White Horse', rendered the more conspicuous by a stone statue of some rampacious animal with flowing mane and tail, distantly resembling an insane cart-horse, which is elevated above the principal door. The Great White Horse is famous in the neighbourhood, in the same degree as a prize ox, or county paper-chronicled turnip, or unwieldy pig – for its enormous size. Never were such labyrinths of uncarpeted passages, such clusters of mouldy, badly-lighted rooms, such huge numbers of small dens for eating or sleeping in, beneath any one roof, as are collected together between the four walls of the Great White Horse at Ipswich.

It was at the door of this overgrown tavern, that the London coach stopped, at the same hour every evening; and it was from this same London coach, that Mr Pickwick, Sam Weller, and Mr Peter Magnus dismounted, on the particular evening to which this chapter of our history bears reference.

'Do you stop here, Sir?' inquired Mr Peter Magnus, when the striped bag, and the red bag, and the brown paper parcel, and the leather hat-box, had all been deposited in the passage. 'Do you stop here, Sir?'

'I do,' said Mr Pickwick.

'Dear me,' said Mr Magnus, 'I never knew anything like these extraordinary coincidences. Why, I stop here, too. I hope we dine together?'

'With pleasure,' replied Mr Pickwick. 'I am not quite certain whether I have any friends here or not, though. Is there any gentleman of the name of Tupman here, waiter?'

A corpulent man, with a fortnight's napkin under his arm,

and coeval stockings on his legs, slowly desisted from his occupation of staring down the street, on this question being put
to him by Mr Pickwick; and, after minutely inspecting that
gentleman's appearance, from the crown of his hat to the lowest
button of his gaiters, replied emphatically –

'No.'

'Nor any gentleman of the name of Snodgrass?' inquired Mr
Pickwick.

'No!'

'Nor Winkle?'

'No.'

'My friends have not arrived to-day, Sir,' said Mr Pickwick.
'We will dine alone, then. Shew us a private room, waiter.'

On this request being preferred, the corpulent man condes-
cended to order the boots to bring in the gentlemen's luggage,
and preceding them down a long dark passage, ushered them
into a large badly-furnished apartment, with a dirty grate, in
which a small fire was making a wretched attempt to be cheerful,
but was fast sinking beneath the dispiriting influence of the
place. After the lapse of an hour, a bit of fish and a steak, were
served up to the travellers, and when the dinner was cleared
away, Mr Pickwick and Mr Peter Magnus drew their chairs up
to the fire, and having ordered a bottle of the worst possible
port wine, at the highest possible price, for the good of the
house, drank brandy and water for their own.

CHARLES DICKENS
from *The Pickwick Papers*

The Tale of the Two Mice

Once on a time (so runs the Fable)
A Country Mouse, right hospitable,
Receiv'd a Town Mouse at his Board,
Just as a Farmer might a Lord.

A frugal Mouse upon the whole,
Yet lov'd his Friend, and had a Soul;
Knew what was handsome, and wou'd do't,
On just occasion, *coute qui coute*.
He brought him Bacon (nothing lean)
Pudding, that might have pleas'd a Dean;
Cheese, such as men in Suffolk make,
But wish'd it Stilton for his sake;
Yet to his Guest tho' no way sparing,
He eat himself the Rind and paring.
Our Courtier scarce could touch a bit,
But show'd his Breeding, and his Wit,
He did his best to seem to eat,
And cry'd, 'I vow you're mighty neat.
As sweet a Cave as one shall see!
A most Romantic hollow Tree!
A pretty kind of savage Scene!
But come, for God's sake, live with Men:
Consider, Mice, like Men, must die,
Both small and great, both you and I:
Then spend your life in Joy and Sport,
(This doctrine, Friend, I learnt at Court.)'
The veriest Hermit in the Nation
May yield, God knows, to strong Temptation.
Away they come, thro thick and thin,
To a tall house near Lincoln's-Inn:

('Twas on the night of a Debate,
When all their Lordships had sate late.)
  Behold the place, where if a Poet
Shin'd in Description, he might show it,
Tell how the Moon-beam trembling falls
And tips with silver all the walls:
Palladian walls, Venetian doors,
Grotesco roofs, and Stucco floors:
But let it (in a word) be said,
The Moon was up, and Men a-bed,
The Napkins white, the Carpet red:
The Guests withdrawn had left the Treat,
And down the Mice sate, *tête à tête.*
  Our Courtier walks from dish to dish,
Tastes for his Friend of Fowl and Fish;
Tells all their names, lays down the law,
'*Que ça est bon! Ah goutez ça!*
That Jelly's rich, this Malmsey healing,
Pray dip your Whiskers and your Tail in'.
Was ever such a happy Swain?
He stuffs and swills, and stuffs again.
'I'm quite asham'd – 'tis mighty rude
To eat so much – but all's so good.
I have a thousand thanks to give –
My Lord alone knows how to live'.
  No sooner said, but from the Hall
Rush Chaplain, Butler, Dogs and all:
'A Rat, a Rat! clap to the door' –
The Cat comes bouncing on the floor.
O for the Heart of Homer's Mice,
Or Gods to save them in a trice!
(It was by Providence, they think,
For your damn'd Stucco has no chink)

'An't please your Honour, quoth the Peasant,
This same Dessert is not so pleasant:
Give me again my hollow Tree!
A Crust of Bread, and Liberty.'

ALEXANDER POPE

School during Wartime

Mrs Bowlby was a kind, silly woman with a peculiar proclivity for *gaffes* which, repeated and exaggerated, formed part of the lore of the school. It may be that this weakness of hers counted against her husband when he was considered for preferment. She gave us tea that afternoon in her drawing-room and said nothing more memorable than that it was a 'patriotic' tea; we could eat with a good conscience because none of the cakes contained flour; some were made of potatoes, some of rice.

This theme of famine, which was to assume large importance in the next eighteen months, was almost new to me. As a treat before going to school I had been taken to hear Harry Lauder, the Scotch music-hall comedian, who after his songs had addressed us on the subject. 'When you cut yourself another slice of bread,' he had declaimed, 'look at the knife. There's blood on it. The blood of a British soldier you have stabbed in the back.' The papers were full of warnings that only voluntary self-denial could save the country from the shame we had so much derided in the Germans, State control of food, but neither at home nor at Heath Mount had there been any shortages. It was in 1917 that the submarine blockade became effective. Adolescents were not as tenderly treated by the rationing authorities of the first war as of the second; my introduction to public-school life coincided with my first experience of hunger.

Mrs Bowlby's patriotic fare was the best I was to enjoy until the summer holidays . . .

The food in Hall would have provoked mutiny in a mid-Victorian poor-house and it grew steadily worse until the end of the war. In happier times it was supplemented from the Grub Shop and by hampers from home. In 1917–18 it afforded a bare subsistence without any pretence to please. There was, I recall, a horrible substance named 'Honey-Sugar', a sort of sweetened cheeselike matter, the by-product of heaven knows what chemical ingenuity, which appeared twice a week at supper in cardboard pots. There was milkless cocoa and small pats of margarine and limitless bread. At midday dinner there was usually a stew consisting chiefly of swedes and potatoes in their skins. Perhaps the table-manners were an unconscious protest against this prison diet. Clean cloths were laid on Sunday; by Tuesday they were filthy. Boys from perfectly civilised homes seemed to glory in savagery and it was this more than the wretched stuff they slopped about which disgusted me. Exceptionally accomplished boys were able to flick pats of margarine from their knives to the high oak rafters overhead, where they stuck all the winter until released by the summer heat they fell, plomp, on the tables below.

EVELYN WAUGH
from *A Little Learning*

'Happie is he, that from all Businesse cleere'

Happie is he, that from all Businesse cleere,
    As the old race of Mankind were,
With his owne Oxen tills his Sires left lands,
    And is not in the Usurers bands:

Nor Souldier-like started with rough alarmes,
　　Nor dreads the Seas inraged harmes:
But flees the Barre and Courts, with the proud bords,
　　And waiting Chambers of great Lords.
The Poplar tall, he then doth marrying twine
　　With the growne issue of the Vine;
And with his hooke lops off the fruitlesse race,
　　And sets more happy in the place:
Or in the bending Vale beholds a-farre
　　The lowing herds there grazing are:
Or the prest honey in pure pots doth keepe
　　Of Earth, and sheares the tender Sheepe:
Or when that Autumne, through the fields, lifts round
　　His head, with mellow Apples crown'd,
How plucking Peares, his owne hand grafted had,
　　And purple-matching Grapes, hee's glad!
With which, Priapus, he may thanke thy hands,
　　And, Sylvane, thine, that keptst his Lands!

Then now beneath some ancient Oke he may,
　　Now in the rooted Grasse him lay,
Whilst from the higher Bankes doe slide the floods;
　　The soft birds quarrell in the Woods,
The Fountaines murmure as the streames doe creepe,
　　And all invite to easie sleepe.
Then when the thundring Jove his Snow and showres
　　Are gathering by the Wintry houres;
Or hence, or thence, he drives with many a Hound
　　Wild Bores into his toyles pitch'd round:
Or straines on his small forke his subtill nets
　　For th' eating Thrush, or Pit-falls sets:

And snares the fearfull Hare, and new-come Crane,
    And 'counts them sweet rewards so ta'en.
Who (amongst these delights) would not forget
    Love cares so evil, and so great?
But if, to boot with these, a chaste Wife meet
    For houshold aid, and Children sweet;
Such as the Sabines, or a Sun-burnt-blowse,
    Some lustie quick Apulians spouse,
To deck the hallow'd Harth with old wood fir'd
    Against the Husband comes home tir'd;
That penning the glad flock in hurdles by,
    Their swelling udders doth draw dry:
And from the sweet Tub Wine of this yeare takes,
    And unbought viands ready makes:
Not Lucrine Oysters I could then more prize,
    Nor Turbot, nor bright Golden-eyes:
If with bright floods, the Winter troubled much,
    Into our Seas send any such:
Th' Ionian God-wit, nor the Ginny hen
    Could not goe downe my belly then
More sweet then Olives, that new gather'd be
    From fattest branches of the Tree:
Or the herb Sorrell, that loves Meadows still,
    Or Mallowes loosing bodyes ill:
Or at the Feast of Bounds, the Lambe then slaine,
    Or Kid forc't from the Wolfe againe.
Among these Cates how glad the sight doth come
    Of the fed flocks approaching home!
To view the weary Oxen draw, with bare
    And fainting necks, the turned Share!
The wealthy houshold swarme of bondmen met,
    And 'bout the steeming Chimney set!

These thoughts when Usurer Alphius, now about
　　To turne mere farmer, had spoke out,
’Gainst th’ Ides, his moneys he gets in with paine,
　　At th’ Calends, puts all out againe.

BEN JONSON

The Pâtés Seller

Before I had got half-way down the street, I changed my mind:
as I am at Versailles, thought I, I might as well take a view of
the town; so I pulled the cord, and ordered the coachman to
drive round some of the principal streets – I suppose the town
is not very large, said I. – The coachman begged pardon for
setting me right, and told me it was very superb, and that
numbers of the first dukes and marquises and counts had hôtels
– The Count de B**** of whom the bookseller at the Quai de
Conti had spoke so handsomely the night before, came instantly
into my mind. – And why should I not go, thought I, to the
Count de B****, who has so high an idea of English books, and
Englishmen, and tell him my story? so I changed my mind a
second time – In truth it was the third; for I had intended that
day for Madame de R**** in the Rue St Pierre, and had devoutly
sent her word by her *fille de chambre* that I would assuredly
wait upon her – but I am governed by circumstances – I cannot
govern them: so seeing a man standing with a basket on the
other side of the street, as if he had something to sell, I bid La
Fleur go up to him and inquire for the Count’s hôtel.

La Fleur returned a little pale; and told me it was a Chevalier
de St Louis selling *pâtés* – It is impossible, La Fleur! said I. – La
Fleur could no more account for the phenomenon than myself;
but persisted in his story: he had seen the croix set in gold, with
its red ribband, he said, tied to his button-hole – and had looked

into the basket, and seen the *pâtés* which the Chevalier was selling; so could not be mistaken in that.

Such a reverse in man's life awakens a better principle than curiosity: I could not help looking for some time at him, as I sat in the *remise* – the more I looked at him, his croix, and his basket, the stronger they wove themselves into my brain – I got out of the *remise* and went towards him.

He was begirt with a clean linen apron which fell below his knees, and with a sort of a bib that went half-way up his breast; upon the top of this, but a little below the hem, hung his croix. His basket of little *pâtés* was covered over with a white damask napkin; another of the same kind was spread at the bottom; and there was a look of *propreté* and neatness throughout, that one might have bought his *pâtés* of him, as much from appetite as sentiment.

He made an offer of them to neither; but stood still with them at the corner of a *hôtel*, for those to buy who chose it without solicitation.

He was about forty-eight – of a sedate look, something approaching to gravity. – I did not wonder. – I went up rather to the basket than him, and having lifted up the napkin, and taken one of his *pâtés* into my hand – I begged he would explain the appearance which affected me.

He told me in a few words, that the best part of his life had passed in the service, in which, after spending a small patrimony, he had obtained a company and the croix with it; but that at the conclusion of the last peace, his regiment being reformed, and the whole corps, with those of some other regiments, left without any provision, he found himself in a wide world without friends, without a livre – and indeed, said he, without any thing but this – (pointing, as he said it, to his croix) – The poor chevalier won my pity, and he finished the scene with winning my esteem too.

The king, he said, was the most generous of princes, but his generosity could neither relieve or reward every one, and it was only his misfortune to be amongst the number. He had a little wife, he said, whom he loved, who did the *patisserie*; and added, he felt no dishonour in defending her and himself from want in this way – unless Providence had offered him a better.

It would be wicked to withhold a pleasure from the good, in passing over what happened to this poor Chevalier of St Louis about nine months after.

It seems he usually took his stand near the iron gates which lead up to the palace, and as his croix had caught the eye of numbers, numbers had made the same inquiry which I had done – He had told them the same story, and always with so much modesty and good sense, that it had reached at last the king's ears – who hearing the chevalier had been a gallant officer, and respected by the whole regiment as a man of honour and integrity – he broke up his little trade by a pension of fifteen hundred livres a year.

LAURENCE STERNE
from *A Sentimental Journey*

The Haschish

Of all that Orient lands can vaunt
  Of marvels with our own competing,
The strangest is the Haschish plant,
  And what will follow on its eating.

What pictures to the taster rise,
  Of Dervish or of Almeh dances!
Of Eblis, or of Paradise,
  Set all aglow with Houri glances!

The poppy visions of Cathay,
   The heavy beer-trance of the Suabian;
The wizard lights and demon play
   Of nights Walpurgis and Arabian!

The Mollah and the Christian dog
   Change place in mad metempsychosis;
The Muezzin climbs the synagogue,
   The Rabbi shakes his beard at Moses!

The Arab by his desert well
   Sits choosing from some Caliph's daughters,
And hears his single camel's bell
   Sound welcome to his regal quarters.

The Koran's reader makes complaint
   Of Shitan dancing on and off it;
The robber offers alms, the saint
   Drinks Tokay and blasphemes the Prophet.

Such scenes that Eastern plant awakes;
   But we have one ordained to beat it,
The Haschish of the West, which makes
   Or fools or knaves of all who eat it.

The preacher eats, and straight appears
   His Bible in a new translation;
Its angels negro overseers,
   And Heaven itself a snug plantation!

The man of peace, about whose dreams
   The sweet millennial angels cluster,
Tastes the mad weed, and plots and schemes,
   A raving Cuban filibuster!

The noisiest Democrat, with ease,
  It turns to Slavery's parish beadle;
The shrewdest statesman eats and sees
  Due southward point the polar needle.

The Judge partakes, and sits erelong
  Upon his bench a railing blackguard;
Decides off-hand that right is wrong,
  And reads the ten commandments backward.

O potent plant! so fare a taste
  Has never Turk or Gentoo gotten;
The hempen Haschish of the East
  Is powerless to our Western Cotton!

JOHN GREENLEAF WHITTIER

Hunger and Poverty

You discover, for instance, the secrecy attaching to poverty. At
a sudden stroke you have been reduced to an income of six
francs a day. But of course you dare not admit it – you have
got to pretend that you are living quite as usual. From the start
it tangles you in a net of lies, and even with the lies you can
hardly manage it. You stop sending clothes to the laundry, and
the laundress catches you in the street and asks you why; you
mumble something, and she, thinking you are sending the
clothes elsewhere, is your enemy for life. The tobacconist keeps
asking why you have cut down your smoking. There are letters
you want to answer, and cannot, because stamps are too expensive. And then there are your meals – meals are the worst
difficulty of all. Every day at meal-times you go out, ostensibly
to a restaurant, and loaf an hour in the Luxembourg Gardens,

watching the pigeons. Afterwards you smuggle your food home in your pockets. Your food is bread and margarine, or bread and wine, and even the nature of the food is governed by lies. You have to buy rye bread instead of household bread, because the rye loaves, though dearer, are round and can be smuggled in your pockets. This wastes you a franc a day. Sometimes, to keep up appearances, you have to spend sixty centimes on a drink, and go correspondingly short of food. Your linen gets filthy, and you run out of soap and razor-blades. Your hair wants cutting, and you try to cut it yourself, with such fearful results that you have to go to the barber after all, and spend the equivalent of a day's food. All day you are telling lies, and expensive lies.

You discover the extreme precariousness of your six francs a day. Mean disasters happen and rob you of food. You have spent your last eighty centimes on half a litre of milk, and are boiling it over the spirit lamp. While it boils a bug runs down your forearm; you give the bug a flick with your nail, and it falls plop! straight into the milk. There is nothing for it but to throw the milk away and go foodless.

You go to the baker's to buy a pound of bread, and you wait while the girl cuts a pound for another customer. She is clumsy, and cuts more than a pound. 'Pardon, monsieur,' she says, 'I suppose you don't mind paying two sous extra?' Bread is a franc a pound, and you have exactly a franc. When you think that you too might be asked to pay two sous extra, and would have to confess that you could not, you bolt in panic. It is hours before you dare venture into a baker's shop again.

You go to the greengrocer's to spend a franc on a kilogram of potatoes. But one of the pieces that make up the franc is a Belgian piece, and the shopman refuses it. You slink out of the shop, and can never go there again.

You have strayed into a respectable quarter, and you see a prosperous friend coming. To avoid him you dodge into the nearest café. Once in the café you must buy something, so you spend your last fifty centimes on a glass of black coffee with a dead fly in it. One could multiply these disasters by the hundred. They are part of the process of being hard up.

You discover what it is like to be hungry. With bread and margarine in your belly, you go out and look into the shop windows. Everywhere there is food insulting you in huge, wasteful piles; whole dead pigs, baskets of hot loaves, great yellow blocks of butter, strings of sausages, mountains of potatoes, vast Gruyère cheeses like grindstones. A snivelling self-pity comes over you at the sight of so much food. You plan to grab a loaf and run, swallowing it before they catch you; and you refrain, from pure funk.

GEORGE ORWELL
from *Down and Out in Paris and London*

Ode on the Death of a Favourite Cat, Drowned in a Tub of Gold Fishes

'Twas on a lofty vase's side,
Where China's gayest art had dyed
    The azure flowers, that blow;
Demurest of the tabby kind,
The pensive Selima reclined,
    Gazed on the lake below.

Her conscious tail her joy declared;
The fair round face, the snowy beard,
    The velvet of her paws,
Her coat, that with the tortoise vies,
Her ears of jet, and emerald eyes,
    She saw; and purred applause.

Still had she gazed; but 'midst the tide
Two angel forms were seen to glide,
    The genii of the stream:
Their scaly armour's Tyrian hue
Through richest purple to the view
    Betrayed a golden gleam.

The hapless nymph with wonder saw:
A whisker first and then a claw,
    With many an ardent wish,
She stretched in vain to reach the prize.
What female heart can gold despise?
    What cat's averse to fish?

Presumptuous maid! with looks intent
Again she stretched, again she bent,
    Nor knew the gulf between.
(Malignant Fate sat by, and smiled)
The slippery verge her feet beguiled,
    She tumbled headlong in.

Eight times emerging from the flood
She mewed to every watery god,
    Some speedy aid to send.
No dolphin came, no Nereid stirred:
Nor cruel Tom, nor Susan heard.
    A favourite has no friend!

From hence, ye beauties, undeceived,
Know, one false step is ne'er retrieved,
    And be with caution bold.

Not all that tempts your wandering eyes
And heedless hearts, is lawful prize;
Nor all that glisters gold.

THOMAS GRAY

Journeyman Meals

At the head of the long, solid oak table sat 'the mistress' with an immense dish of meat before her, carving knife in hand. Then came a reserved space, sometimes occupied by visitors, but more often blank table-cloth; then Matthew's chair, and, after that, another, smaller blank space, just sufficient to mark the difference in degree between a foreman and ordinary workmen. Beyond that, the three young men sat in a row at the end of the table, facing the mistress. Zillah, the maid, had a little round table to herself by the wall. Unless important visitors were present, she joined freely in the conversation; but the three young men seldom opened their mouths excepting to shovel in food. If, by chance, they had something they thought of sufficient interest to impart, they always addressed their remarks to Miss Lane, and prefixed them by 'Ma-am'. 'Ma-am, have you heard that Squire Bashford's sold his Black Beauty?' or 'Ma-am, I've heard say that two ricks've bin burnt down at Wheeler's. A tramp sleeping under set 'em afire, they think.' But, usually, the only sound at their end of the table was that of the scraping of plates, or of a grunt of protest if one of them nudged another too suddenly. They had special cups and saucers, very large and thick, and they drank their beer out of horns, instead of glasses or mugs. There were certain small delicacies on the table which were never offered them and which they took obvious pains not to appear to notice. When they had finished their always excellent meal, one of them said 'Pardon, Ma-am,' and they all tip-toed out. Then Zillah brought in the tea-tray and Matthew stayed for a cup before he, too, withdrew. At tea-time they all had tea to drink, but Miss Lane said this was an innovation of her own. In her father's time the family had tea alone, it was their one private meal, and the men had what was called 'afternoon bavour', which consisted of bread and cheese and beer, at three o'clock.

As a child, Laura thought the young men were poorly treated and was inclined to pity them; but, afterwards, she found they were under an age-old discipline, supposed, in some mysterious way, to fit them for becoming in their turn master-men. Under this system, such and such an article of food was not suitable for the men; the men must have something substantial – boiled beef and dumplings, or a thick cut off a gammon, or a joint of beef. When they came in to go to bed on a cold night, they could be offered hot spiced beer, but not elderberry wine. They must not be encouraged to talk and you must never discuss family affairs in their presence, or they might become familiar; in short, they must be kept in their place, because they were 'the men'.

Until that time, or a few years earlier in more advanced districts, these distinctions had suited the men as well as they had done the employers. Their huge meals and their beds in a row in the large attic were part of their wages, and as long as it was excellent food and the beds were good feather beds with plenty of blankets, they had all they expected or wished for indoors. More would have embarrassed them. They had their own lives outside.

FLORA THOMPSON
from *Candleford Green*

Eggs

He walked between two coal wagons and out over a dusty expanse of street towards yellow streetcars. A trembling took hold of his knees. He thrust his hands deep in his pockets.

EAT on a lunchwagon halfway down the block. He slid stiffly onto a revolving stool and looked for a long while at the pricelist.

'Fried eggs and a cup o coffee.'

'Want 'em turned over?' asked the redhaired man behind the counter who was wiping off his beefy freckled forearms with his apron. Bud Korpenning sat up with a start.

'What?'

'The eggs? Want 'em turned over or sunny side up?'

'Oh sure, turn 'em over.' Bud slouched over the counter again with his head between his hands.

'You look all in, feller,' the man said as he broke the eggs into the sizzling grease of the frying pan.

'Came down from upstate. I walked fifteen miles this mornin.'

The man made a whistling sound through his eyeteeth. 'Comin to the big city to look for a job, eh?'

Bud nodded. The man flopped the eggs sizzling and netted with brown out onto the plate and pushed it towards Bud with some bread and butter on the edge of it. 'I'm going to slip you a bit of advice, feller, and it won't cost you nutten. You go an git a shave and a haircut and brush the hayseeds out o yer suit a bit before you start lookin. You'll be more likely to git somethin. It's looks that count in this city.'

'I kin work all right. I'm a good worker,' growled Bud with his mouth full.

'I'm telling yez, that's all,' said the redhaired man and turned back to his stove.

JOHN DOS PASSOS
from *Manhattan Transfer*

Eden

That day, as other solemn days, they spent
In song and dance about the sacred hill,
Mystical dance, which yonder starry sphere
Of planets and of fixed in all her wheels
Resembles nearest, mazes intricate,
Eccentric, intervolved, yet regular
Then most, when most irregular they seem,
And in their motions harmony divine
So smooths her charming tones, that God's own ear
Listens delighted. Ev'ning now approached
(For we have also our ev'ning and our morn,
We ours for change delectable, not need);
Forthwith from dance to sweet repast they turn
Desirous; all in circles as they stood,
Tables are set, and on a sudden piled
With angels' food, and rubied nectar flows
In pearl, in diamond, and massy gold,
Fruit of delicious vines, the growth of Heav'n.
On flow'rs reposed, and with fresh flow'rets crowned,
They eat, they drink, and in communication sweet
Quaff immortality and joy, secure
Of surfeit where full measure only bounds
Excess, before th' all bounteous King, who show'red
With copious hand, rejoicing in their joy.

JOHN MILTON
from *Paradise Lost*

The Tempter and Eve

As when of old some Orator renown'd
In Athens or free Rome, where Eloquence
Flourish'd, since mute, to some great cause addrest,
Stood in himself collected, while each part,
Motion, each act won audience ere the tongue,
Sometimes in heighth began, as no delay
Of Preface brooking through his Zeal of Right.
So standing, moving, or to heighth upgrown
The Tempter all impassion'd thus began.
    'O Sacred, Wise, and Wisdom-giving Plant,
Mother of Science, Now I feel thy Power
Within me clear, not only to discern
Things in their Causes, but to trace the ways
Of highest Agents, deem'd however wise.
Queen of this Universe, do not believe
Those rigid threats of Death; ye shall not Die:
How should ye? by the Fruit? it gives you Life
To Knowledge: By the Threat'ner? look on mee,
Mee who have touch'd and tasted, yet both live,
And life more perfect have attain'd than Fate
Meant mee, by vent'ring higher than my Lot.
Shall that be shut to Man, which to the Beast
Is open? or will God incense his ire
For such a petty Trespass, and not praise
Rather your dauntless virtue, whom the pain
Of Death denounc't, whatever thing Death be,
Deterr'd not from achieving what might lead
To happier life, knowledge of Good and Evil;
Of good, how just? of evil, if what is evil
Be real, why not known, since easier shunn'd?
God therefore cannot hurt ye, and be just;

Not just, not God; not fear'd then, nor obey'd:
Your fear itself of Death removes the fear.
Why then was this forbid? Why but to awe,
Why but to keep ye low and ignorant,
His worshippers; he knows that in the day
Ye Eat thereof, your Eyes that seem so clear,
Yet are but dim, shall perfectly be then
Op'n'd and clear'd, and ye shall be as Gods,
Knowing both Good and Evil as they know.
That ye should be as Gods, since I as Man,
Internal Man, is but proportion meet,
I of brute human, yee of human Gods.
So ye shall die perhaps, by putting off
Human, to put on Gods, death to be wisht,
Though threat'n'd, which no worse than this can bring.
And what are Gods that Man may not become
As they, participating God-like food?
The Gods are first, and that advantage use
On our belief, that all from them proceeds;
I question it, for this fair Earth I scc,
Warm'd by the Sun, producing every kind,
Them nothing: If they all things, who enclos'd
Knowledge of Good and Evil in this Tree,
That whoso eats thereof, forthwith attains
Wisdom without their leave? and wherein lies
Th'offence, that Man should thus attain to know?
What can your knowledge hurt him, or this Tree
Impart against his will if all be his?
Or is it envy, and can envy dwell
In heav'nly breasts? these, these and many more
Causes import your need of this fair Fruit.
Goddess humane, reach then, and freely taste.'
    He ended, and his words replete with guile
Into her heart too easy entrance won:

Fixt on the Fruit she gaz'd, which to behold
Might tempt alone, and in her ears the sound
Yet rung of his persuasive words, impregn'd
With Reason, to her seeming, and with Truth;
Meanwhile the hour of Noon drew on, and wak'd
An eager appetite, rais'd by the smell
So savoury of that Fruit, which with desire,
Inclinable now grown to touch or taste,
Solicited her longing eye; yet first
Pausing awhile, thus to herself she mus'd.

 'Great are thy Virtues, doubtless, best of Fruits,
Though kept from Man, and worthy to be admir'd,
Whose taste, too long forborne, at first assay
Gave elocution to the mute, and taught
The Tongue not made for Speech to speak thy praise:
Thy praise hee also who forbids thy use,
Conceals not from us, naming thee the Tree
Of Knowledge, knowledge both of good and evil;
Forbids us then to taste, but his forbidding
Commends thee more, while it infers the good
By thee communicated, and our want:
For good unknown, sure is not had, or had
And yet unknown, is as not had at all.
In plain then, what forbids he but to know,
Forbids us good, forbids us to be wise?
Such prohibitions bind not. But if Death
Bind us with after-bands, what profits then
Our inward freedom? In the day we eat
Of this fair Fruit, our doom is, we shall die.
How dies the Serpent? hee hath eat'n and lives,
And knows, and speaks, and reasons, and discerns,
Irrational till then. For us alone
Was death invented? or to us deni'd
This intellectual food, for beasts reserv'd?

For Beasts it seems: yet that one Beast which first
Hath tasted, envies not, but brings with joy
The good befall'n him, Author unsuspect,
Friendly to man, far from deceit or guile.
What fear I then, rather what know to fear
Under this ignorance of Good and Evil,
Of God or Death, of Law or Penalty?
Here grows the Cure of all, this Fruit Divine,
Fair to the Eye, inviting to the Taste,
Of virtue to make wise: what hinders then
To reach, and feed at once both Body and Mind?'
   So saying, her rash hand in evil hour
Forth reaching to the Fruit, she pluck'd, she ate:
Earth felt the wound, and Nature from her seat
Sighing through all her Works gave signs of woe,
That all was lost. Back to the Thicket slunk
The guilty Serpent, and well might, for Eve
Intent now wholly on her taste, naught else
Regarded, such delight till then, as seem'd,
In Fruit she never tasted, whether true
Or fancied so, through expectation high
Of knowledge, nor was Godhead from her thought.
Greedily she ingorg'd without restraint,
And knew not eating Death . . .

JOHN MILTON
from *Paradise Lost*

'Boy, I hate their empty shows'

Boy, I hate their empty shows,
   Persian garlands I detest,
Bring not me the late-blown rose
   Ling'ring after all the rest:

Plainer myrtle pleases me
   Thus out-stretch'd beneath my vine,
Myrtle more becoming thee,
   Waiting with thy master's wine.

WILLIAM COWPER

'Ah child, no Persian – perfect art!'

Ah child, no Persian – perfect art!
Crowns composite and braided bast
They tease me. Never know the part
   Where roses linger last.

Bring natural myrtle, and have done:
Myrtle will suit your place and mine:
And set the glasses from the sun
   Beneath the tackled vine.

GERARD MANLEY HOPKINS

Gluttony and Drunkenness

The Complaint of Gluttony

The Roman emperors that succeeded Augustus were exceedingly given to this horrible vice, whereof some of them would feed on nothing but the tongues of pheasants and nightingales; others would spend as much at one banquet as a king's revenues came to in a year; whose excess I would decipher at large, but that a new laureate hath saved me the labour, who, for a man that stands upon pains and not wit, hath performed as much as any story-dresser may do, that sets a new English nap on an old Latin apophthegm. It is enough for me to lick dishes here at home, though I feed not mine eyes at any of the Roman feasts. Much good do it you, Master Dives, here in London; for you are he my pen means to dine withal. *Miserere mei*, what a fat churl it is! Why, he hath a belly as big as the round church in Cambridge, a face as huge as the whole body of a base viol, and legs that, if they were hollow, a man might keep a mill in either of them. *Experto crede, Roberto*, there is no mast like a merchant's table. *Bona fide*, it is a great misture, that we have not men swine as well as beasts, for then we should have pork that hath no more bones than a pudding and a side of bacon that you might lay under your head instead of a bolster.

*Nature in England is but Plain Dame, but in Spain and Italy,
because they have more use of her than we, she is dubbed
a Lady*

It is not for nothing that other countries, whom we upbraid with drunkenness, call us bursten-bellied gluttons; for we make our greedy paunches powdering-tubs of beef, and eat more meat at one meal than the Spaniard or Italian in a month. Good thrifty men, they draw out a dinner with sallets, like a

Swart-rutter's suit, and make *Madonna* Nature their best caterer. We must have our tables furnished like poulters' stalls, or as though we were to victual Noah's ark again wherein there was all sorts of living creatures that ever were, or else the good-wife will not open her mouth to bid one welcome. A stranger that should come to one of our *magnificoes*' houses, when dinner were set on the board, and he not yet set, would think the goodman of the house were a haberdasher of wildfowl, or a merchant venturer of dainty meat, that sells commodity of good cheer by the great, and hath factors in Arabia, Turkey, Egypt, and Barbary, to provide him of strange birds, China mustard, and odd patterns to make custards by.

Lord, what a coil we have, with this course and that course, removing this dish higher, setting another lower, and taking away the third. A general might in less space remove his camp, than they stand disposing of their gluttony. And whereto tends all this gourmandise, but to give sleep gross humours to feed on, to corrupt the brain, and make it unapt and unwieldy for anything?

The Roman censors, if they lighted upon a fat corpulent man, they straight away took away his horse, and constrained him to go afoot; positively concluding his carcase was so puffed up with gluttony or idleness. If we had such horse-takers amongst us, and that surfeit-swollen churls, who now ride on their foot-cloths, might be constrained to carry their flesh-budgets from place to place on foot, the price of velvet and cloth would fall with their bellies, and the gentle craft (alias, the red herring's kinsmen) get more and drink less. *Plenus venter nil agit libenter, et plures gula occidit quam gladius.* It is as desperate a piece of service to sleep upon a full stomach as it is to serve in face of the bullet; a man is but his breath, and that may as well be stopped by putting too much in his mouth at once, as running on the mouth of the cannon. That is verified of us, which Horace writes of an outrageous eater in his time, *Quicquid quæsierat ventri donabat avaro*; 'whatsoever he could rap or rend, he confiscated to his covetous gut.' Nay, we are such flesh-eating Saracans that chaste fish may not content us, but we delight in the murder of innocent mutton, in the unpluming of pullery, and quartering of calves and oxen. It is horrible and detestable; no godly fishmonger that can digest it.

A Rare Witty Jest of Doctor Watson

Report, which our moderners clep floundering Fame, puts me in memory of a notable jest I heard long ago of Doctor Watson, very conducible to the reproof of these fleshly-minded Belials.* He being at supper on a fasting or fish night at least, with a great number of his friends and acquaintance, there chanced to be in the company an outlandish doctor, who, when all other fell to such victuals (agreeing to the time) as were before them, he overslipped them, and there being one joint of flesh on the table for such as had weak stomachs, fell freshly to it. After that hunger, half conquered, had restored him to the use of his speech, for his excuse he said to his friend that brought him thither, '*Profecto, Domine, ego sum malissimus piscator*,' meaning by *piscator*, a fishman (which is a liberty, as also *Malissimus*, that outlandish men in their familiar talk do challenge, at least above us). '*At tu es bonissimus carnifex*,' quoth Doctor Watson, retorting very merrily his own licentious figures upon him. So of us may it be said, we are *malissimi piscatores*, but *bonissimi carnifices*. I would English the jest for the edification of the temporality, but that it is not so good in English as in Latin; and though it were as good, it would not convert clubs and clouted shoon from the flesh pots of Egypt to the provant of the Low Countries; for they had rather (with the servingman) put up a supplication to the Parliament House that they might

---

* Or rather Belly-alls, because all their mind is on their belly.

have a yard of pudding for a penny, than desire (with the baker)
there might be three ounces of bread sold for a halfpenny.

The Moderation of Friar Alphonso, King Philip's Confessor

Alphonsus, King Philip's confessor, that came over with him to
England, was such a moderate man in his diet, that he would
feed but once a day, and at that time he would feed so slenderly
and sparingly, as scarce served to keep life and soul together.
One night, importunately invited to a solemn banquet, for
fashion sake he sat down among the rest, but by no entreaty
could be drawn to eat anything. At length, fruit being set on
the board, he reached an apple out of the dish and put it in his
pocket, which one marking, that sat right over against him,
asked him, '*Domine, cur es solicitus in crastinum?* – Sir, why are
you careful for the morrow?' Whereto he answered most soberly,
'*Immo hoc facio, mi amice, ut ne sim solicitus in crastinum.* No,
I do it, my friend, that I may not be careful for the morrow.'
As though his appetite were a whole day contented with so little
as an apple, and that it were enough to pay the morrow's tribute
to nature.

The Strange Alteration of the County Molines, the Prince of Parma's Companion

Rare, and worthy to be registered to all posterities, is the County
Moline's (sometime the Prince of Parma's companion) altered
course of life, who, being a man that lived in as great pomp and
delicacy as was possible for a man to do, and one that wanted
nothing but a kingdom that his heart could desire, upon a day
entering into a deep melancholy by himself, he fell into a
discursive consideration what this world was, how vain and
transitory the pleasures thereof, and how many times he had
offended God by surfeiting, gluttony, drunkenness, pride,
whoredom, and such like, and how hard it was for him, that

lived in that prosperity that he did, not to be entangled with those pleasures. Whereupon he presently resolved, twixt God and his own conscience, to forsake it and all his allurements, and betake him to the severest form of life used in their state. And with that called his soldiers and acquaintance together, and, making known his intent unto them, he distributed his living and possessions, which were infinite, amongst the poorest of them; and having not left himself the worth of one farthing under heaven, betook him to the most beggarly new erected Order of the Friar Capuchines. Their institution is, that they shall possess nothing whatsoever of their own more than the clothes on their backs, continually to go barefoot, wear hair shirts, and lie upon the hard boards, winter and summer time. They must have no meat, nor ask any but what is given them voluntarily, nor must they lay up any from meal to meal, but give it to the poor, or else it is a great penalty. In this severe humility lives this devout County, and hath done this twelvemonth, submitting himself to all the base drudgery of the house, as fetching water, making clean the rest of their chambers, insomuch as he is the junior of the order. Oh, what a notable rebuke were his honourable lowliness to succeeding pride, if this prostrate spirit of his were not the servant of superstition, or he mispent not his good works on a wrong faith.

Let but our English belly-gods punish their pursy bodies with this strict penance, and profess Capuchinism but one month, and I'll be their pledge they shall not grow so like dry-fats as they do. Oh, it will make them jolly long-winded, to trot up and down the dorter stairs, and the water-tankard will keep the insurrection of their shoulders, the hair shirt will chase whoredom out of their bones, and the hard lodging on the boards take their flesh down a button-hole lower.

But if they might be induced to distribute all their goods amongst the poor, it were to be hoped Saint Peter would let them dwell in the suburbs of heaven, whereas otherwise they must keep aloof at Pancredge, and not come near the liberties by five leagues and above. It is your doing, Diotrephes Devil, that these stall-fed cormorants to damnation must bung up all the wealth of the land in their snap-hance bags, and poor scholars and soldiers wander in back lanes and the out-shifts of the city, with never a rag to their backs. But our trust is, that by some intemperance or other, you will turn up their heels one of these years together, and provide them of such unthrifts to their heirs, as shall spend in one week amongst good fellows what they got by extortion and oppression from gentlemen all their life-time.

The Complaint of Drunkenness

From gluttony in meats, let me descend to superfluity in drink: a sin that, ever since we have mixed ourselves with the Low Countries, is counted honourable, but, before we knew their lingering wars, was held in the highest degree of hatred that might be. Then, if we had seen a man go wallowing in the streets, or lain sleeping under the board, we would have spit at him as a toad, and called him foul drunken swine, and warned all our friends out of his company. Now, he is nobody that cannot drink *super nagulum*, carouse the hunter's hoop, quaff *upsey freze cross*, with healths, gloves, mumps, frolics, and a thousand such domineering inventions. He is reputed a peasant and a boor that will not take his liquor profoundly. And you shall hear a cavalier of the first feather, a princox that was but a page the other day in the Court, and now is all-to-be-frenchified in his soldier's suit, stand upon terms with 'God's wounds, you dishonour me, sir, you do me the disgrace if you do not pledge me as much as I drunk to you;' and, in the midst of his cups, stand vaunting his manhood, beginning every sentence with, 'When I first bore arms', when he never bare anything but his lord's rapier after him in his life. If he have been over and visited a town of garrison, as a traveller or passenger, he hath as great experience as the greatest commander and chief leader in England. A mighty deformer of men's manners and features is this unnecessary vice of all other. Let him be indued with never so many virtues, and have as much goodly proportion and favour as nature can bestow upon a man, yet if he be thirsty after his own destruction, and hath no joy nor comfort but when he is drowning his soul in a gallon pot, that one beastly imperfection will utterly obscure all that is commendable in him, and all his good qualities sink like lead down to the bottom of his carousing cups, where they will lie like lees and dregs, dead and unregarded of any man.

Clim of the Clough, thou that usest to drink nothing but scalding lead and sulphur in hell, thou art not so greedy of thy night gear. Oh, but thou hast a foul swallow if it come once to carousing of human blood; but that's but seldom, once in seven year, when there's a great execution, otherwise thou art tied at rack and manger, and drinkest nothing but the *aqua vitæ* of vengeance all thy life-time. The proverb gives it forth thou art a knave, and therefore I have more hope thou art some manner of good fellow. Let me entreat thee, since thou hast other iniquities enough to circumvent us withal, to wipe this sin out of the catalogue of thy subtleties; help to blast the vines, that they may bear no more grapes, and sour the wines in the cellars of merchants' store-houses, that our countrymen may not piss out all their wit and thrift against the walls.

King Edgar's Ordinance Against Drinking

King Edgar, because his subjects should not offend in swilling and bibbing, as they did, caused certain iron cups to be chained to every fountain and well's side, and at every vintner's door, with iron pins in them, to stint every man how much he should drink; and he that went beyond one of those pins forfeited a penny for every draught. And, if storie were well searched, I believe hoops in quart pots were invented to that end, that every man should take his hoop, and no more.

The Wonderful Abstinence of the Marquis of Pisana, Yet Living

I have heard it justified for a truth by great personages, that the old Marquis of Pisana, who yet lives, drinks not once in seven year; and I have read of one Andron of Argos, that was so seldom thirsty, that he travelled over the hot, burning sands of Lybia, and never drank. Then why should our cold clime bring forth such fiery throats? Are we more thirsty than Spain and Italy, where the sun's force is doubled? The Germans and Low Dutch, methinks, should be continually kept moist with the foggy air and stinking mists that arise out of their fenny soil; but as their country is over-flown with water, so are their heads always overflown with wine, and in their bellies they have standing quagmires and bogs of English beer.

The Private Laws Amongst Drunkards

One of their breed it was that writ the book *De Arte Bibendi*, a worshipful treatise fit for none but Silenus and his ass to set forth. Besides that volume, we have general rules and injunctions, as good as printed precepts, or statutes set down by Act of Parliament, that go from drunkard to drunkard; as still to keep your first man, not to leave any flocks in the bottom of the cup, to knock the glass on your thumb when you have done, to have some shoeing horn to pull on your wine, as a rasher off the coals or a red herring, to stir it about with a candle's end to make it taste better, and not to hold your peace while the pot is stirring.

The Eight Kinds of Drunkenness

Nor have we one or two kinds of drunkards only, but eight kinds. The first is ape drunk, and he leaps, and sings, and holloes, and danceth for the heavens. The second is lion drunk, and he flings the pots about the house, calls his hostess whore, breaks the glass windows with his dagger, and is apt to quarrel with any man that speaks to him. The third is swine drunk, heavy, lumpish, and sleepy, and cries for a little more drink and a few more clothes. The fourth is sheep drunk, wise in his own conceit when he cannot bring forth a right word. The fifth is maudlin drunk when a fellow will weep for kindness in the midst of his ale, and kiss you, saying, 'By God, captain, I love thee; go thy ways, thou dost not think so often of me as I do of thee; I would (if it pleased God) I could not love thee so well as I do.' And then he puts his finger in his eye and cries. The sixth is martin drunk, when a man is drunk and drinks himself sober ere he stir. The seventh is goat drunk, when, in his drunkenness, he hath no mind but on lechery. The eighth is fox drunk, when he is crafty drunk, as many of the Dutchmen be, that will never bargain but when they are drunk. All these species, and more, I have seen practised in one company at one sitting, when I have been permitted to remain sober amongst them, only to note their several humours. He that plies any one of them hard, it will make him to write admirable verses, and to have a deep casting head, though he were never so very a dunce before.

The Discommodities of Drunkenness

Gentlemen, all you that will not have your brains twice sodden, your flesh rotten with the dropsy, that love not to go in greasy doublets, stockings out at the heels, and wear alehouse daggers at your backs: forswear this slavering bravery, that will make you have stinking breaths, and your bodies smell like brewers' aprons; rather keep a snuff in the bottom of the glass to light you to bed withal, than leave never an eye in your head to lead you over the threshold. It will bring you in your old age to be companions with none but porters and car-men, to talk out of a cage, railing as drunken men are wont, a hundred boys wondering about them; and to die suddenly, as Fol Long the fencer did, drinking *aqua vitæ*. From which (as all the rest) good Lord deliver Pierce Penniless.

THOMAS NASHE
from *Pierce Penniless*

'I asked a thief to steal me a peach'

I asked a thief to steal me a peach:
He turned up his eyes.
I asked a lithe lady to lie her down:
Holy & meek, she cries –

As soon as I went
An angel came.
He wink'd at the thief
And smil'd at the dame.

And without one word said
Had a peach from the tree,
And still as a maid
Enjoy'd the lady.

WILLIAM BLAKE

'You sweep my table: sausages, and chine'

You sweep my table: sausages, and chine,
A capon on which two at least may dine,
Smelts, salmon, sturgeon, birds of every feather,
Dripping with sauce, you wrap up all together;
And give it to your servant home to bear;
Leave us nothing, but to sit and stare.
For shame restore the dinner; ease our sorrow:
I did not ask you, sir, to dine to-morrow.

WILLIAM HAY

'What does the bee do?'

What does the bee do?
Bring home honey.
And what does Father do?
Bring home money.
And what does Mother do?
Lay out the money.
And what does baby do?
Eat up the honey.

CHRISTINA G. ROSSETTI
from *Sing-Song*

Back in Lower Binfield

There's Lovegrove's! And there's Todd's! And a big dark shop with beams and dormer windows. Used to be Lilywhite's the draper's, where Elsie used to work. And Grimmett's! Still a grocer's, apparently. Now for the horse-trough in the market-place. There was another car ahead of me and I couldn't see.

It turned aside as we got into the market-place. The horse-trough was gone.

There was an AA man on traffic-duty where it used to stand. He gave a glance at the car, saw that it hadn't the AA sign and decided not to salute.

I turned the corner and ran down to the George. The horse-trough being gone had thrown me out to such an extent that I hadn't even looked to see whether the brewery chimney was still standing. The George had altered too, all except the name. The front had been dolled up till it looked like one of those riverside hotels, and the sign was different. It was curious that although till that moment I hadn't thought of it once in twenty years, I suddenly found that I could remember every detail of the old sign, which had swung there ever since I could remember. It was a crude kind of picture, with St George on a very thin horse trampling on a very fat dragon, and in the corner, though it was cracked and faded, you could read the little signature, 'Wm Sandford, Painter & Carpenter'. The new sign was kind of artistic-looking. You could see it had been painted by a real artist. St George looked a regular pansy. The cobbled yard, where the farmers' traps used to stand and the drunks used to puke on Saturday nights, had been enlarged to about three times its size and concreted over, with garages all round it. I backed the car into one of the garages and got out.

One thing I've noticed about the human mind is that it goes

in jerks. There's no emotion that stays by you for any length of time. During the last quarter of an hour I'd had what you could fairly describe as a shock. I'd felt it almost like a sock in the guts when I stopped at the top of Chamford Hill and suddenly realised that Lower Binfield had vanished, and there'd been another little stab when I saw that the horse-trough was gone. I'd driven through the streets with a gloomy, Ichabod kind of feeling. But as I stepped out of the car and hitched my trilby hat onto my head I suddenly felt that it didn't matter a damn. It was such a lovely sunny day, and the hotel yard had a kind of summery look, with its flowers in green tubs and what-not. Besides, I was hungry and looking forward to a spot of lunch.

I strolled into the hotel with a consequential kind of air, with the boots, who'd already nipped out to meet me, following with the suitcase. I felt pretty prosperous, and probably I looked it. A solid businessman, you'd have said, at any rate if you hadn't seen the car. I was glad I'd come in my new suit – blue flannel with a thin white stripe, which suits my style. It has what the tailor calls a 'reducing effect'. I believe that day I could have passed for a stockbroker. And say what you like it's a very pleasant thing, on a June day when the sun's shining on the pink geraniums in the window-boxes, to walk into a nice country hotel with roast lamb and mint sauce ahead of you.

Not that it's any treat to me to stay in hotels, Lord knows I see all too much of them – but ninety-nine times out of a hundred it's those godless 'family and commercial' hotels, like Rowbottom's, where I was supposed to be staying at present, the kind of places where you pay five bob for bed and breakfast, and the sheets are always damp and the bath taps never work. The George had got so smart I wouldn't have known it. In the old days it had hardly been a hotel, only a pub, though it had a room or two to let and used to do a farmers' lunch (roast beef and Yorkshire, suet dumpling and Stilton cheese) on market days. It all seemed different except for the public bar, which I got a glimpse of as I went past, and which looked the same as ever. I went up a passage with a soft carpet, and hunting prints and copper warming-pans and such-like junk hanging on the walls. And dimly I could remember the passage as it used to be, the hollowed-out flags underfoot, and the smell of plaster mixed up with the smell of beer.

GEORGE ORWELL
from *Coming Up for Air*

The Night Before the Morning After

So, at a given moment, he resigned himself to the joys of alcohol, wisely telling himself that if there was to be a hateful and repentant morning after the night before, he would at least see that the pleasure of the night before was not marred by the hatefulness of repentance – so that the night before and the morning after, the one in its pleasure, and the other in its pain, might from the true perspective of a long-distance view in time seem to cancel each other out. It was largely a question of time, and Johnnie always thought that if you could only have your morning after first, and your night before afterwards, the whole problem of drinking, and indeed of excess and sin in life generally, would be simplified or solved.

The first thing, of course, for those in the suburbs who realize they are going to get drunk is to hop into a taxi and move towards the West End. This they now did almost without consulting each other. They rose automatically when the round was finished, and took their conquering spirits out into the air.

A taxi was found in the Earl's Court Road and at first they could not decide where they wanted to go. Then Johnnie said he would take them all to eat in a place he knew in Soho, and its address was given to the man. But on the way a discussion of places and pubs arose, and their plans were altered in favour of Shepherd's Market, because of a place which Netta knew about.

Here they had three more rounds, and talked madly at each other. Netta and Johnnie talked about the theatre and its personalities, and Johnnie and George talked about their schooldays and their friends in common. Then they went on to another pub near by and began again. But before they had had two rounds here the lights went down on them and the 'All out' was being called. They rushed a last drink, and made for Oddenino's, where they could have more drinks with sandwiches on the extension.

Periods of slight gloom and dizziness were now overtaking Johnnie, as they always did on a long steady drunk without eats, but he saw that George's spirits were maintained at the same high level. It was as though he attached some enormous significance to this meeting of his two friends, and that he was unable to get over the wonder of it.

When they got to Oddenino's, and were having beer and sandwiches, this enthusiasm of George's reached a sort of peak, and caused a conversation which next morning Johnnie was inclined to regret . . .

PATRICK HAMILTON
from *Hangover Square*

The Franklin

A Frankeleyn was in his compaignye.
Whit was his berd as is the dayesye;
Of his complexioun he was sangwyn.
Wel loved he by the morwe a sop in wyn;
To lyven in delit was evere his wone,
For he was Epicurus owene sone,
That heeld opinioun that pleyn delit
Was verray felicitee parfit.
An housholdere, and that a greet, was he;
Seint Julian he was in his contree.
His breed, his ale, was alweys after oon;
A bettre envyned man was nowher noon.
Withoute bake mete was nevere his hous,
Of fissh and flessh, and that so plentevous
It snewed in his hous of mete and drynke;
Of alle deyntees that men koude thynke,
After the sondry sesons of the yeer,
So chaunged he his mete and his soper.
Ful many a fat partrich hadde he in muwe,
And many a breem and many a luce in stuwe.
Wo was his cook but if his sauce were
Poynaunt and sharp, and redy al his geere.
His table dormant in his halle alway
Stood redy covered al the longe day.

GEOFFREY CHAUCER
from *The General Prologue*

Gatsby's Parties

There was music from my neighbour's house through the summer nights. In his blue gardens men and girls came and went like moths among the whisperings and the champagne and the stars. At high tide in the afternoon I watched his guests diving from the tower of his raft, or taking the sun on the hot sand of his beach while his two motor-boats slit the waters of the Sound, drawing aquaplanes over cataracts of foam. On weekends his Rolls-Royce became an omnibus, bearing parties to and from the city between nine in the morning and long past midnight, while his station wagon scampered like a brisk yellow bug to meet all trains. And on Mondays eight servants, including an extra gardener, toiled all day with mops and scrubbing-brushes and hammers and garden-shears, repairing the ravages of the night before.

Every Friday five crates of oranges and lemons arrived from a fruiterer in New York – every Monday these same oranges and lemons left his back door in a pyramid of pulpless halves. There was a machine in the kitchen which could extract the juice of two hundred oranges in half an hour if a little button was pressed two hundred times by a butler's thumb.

At least once a fortnight a corps of caterers came down with several hundred feet of canvas and enough coloured lights to make a Christmas tree of Gatsby's enormous garden. On buffet tables, garnished with glistening hors-d'œuvre, spiced baked hams crowded against salads of harlequin designs and pastry pigs and turkeys bewitched to a dark gold. In the main hall a bar with a real brass rail was set up, and stocked with gins and liquors and with cordials so long forgotten that most of his female guests were too young to know one from another.

By seven o'clock the orchestra has arrived, no thin five-piece affair, but a whole pitful of oboes and trombones and saxophones and viols and cornets and piccolos, and low and high drums. The last swimmers have come in from the beach now and are dressing upstairs; the cars from New York are parked five deep in the drive, and already the halls and salons and verandas are gaudy with primary colours, and hair bobbed in strange new ways, and shawls beyond the dreams of Castile. The bar is in full swing, and floating rounds of cocktails permeate the garden outside, until the air is alive with chatter and laughter, and casual innuendo and introductions forgotten on the spot, and enthusiastic meetings between women who never knew each other's names.

The lights grow brighter as the earth lurches away from the sun, and now the orchestra is playing yellow cocktail music, and the opera of voices pitches a key higher. Laughter is easier minute by minute, spilled with prodigality, tipped out at a cheerful word. The groups change more swiftly, swell with new arrivals, dissolve and form in the same breath; already there are wanderers, confident girls who weave here and there among the stouter and more stable, become for a sharp, joyous moment the centre of a group, and then, excited with triumph, glide on through the sea-change of faces and voices and colour under the constantly changing light.

Suddenly one of these gypsies, in trembling opal, seizes a cocktail out of the air, dumps it down for courage and, moving her hands like Frisco, dances out alone on the canvas platform. A momentary hush; the orchestra leader varies his rhythm obligingly for her, and there is a burst of chatter as the erroneous news goes around that she is Gilda Gray's understudy from the Follies. The party has begun.

F. SCOTT FITZGERALD
from *The Great Gatsby*

Herba Santa

I

After long wars when comes release
Not olive wands proclaiming peace
   An import dearer share
Than stems of Herba Santa hazed
   In autumn's Indian air.
Of moods they breathe that care disarm,
They pledge us lenitive and calm.

II

Shall code or creed a lure afford
To win all selves to Love's accord?
When Love ordained a supper divine
   For the wide world of man,
What bickerings o'er his gracious wine!
   Then strange new feuds began.

Effectual more in lowlier way,
   Pacific Herb, thy sensuous plea
The bristling clans of Adam sway
   At least to fellowship in thee!
Before thine altar tribal flags are furled,
Fain woulds't thou make one hearthstone of the world.

III

To scythe, to sceptre, pen and hod –
   Yea, sodden laborers dumb;
To brains overplied, to feet that plod,
In solace of the *Truce of God*
   The Calumet has come!

IV

Ah for the world ere Raleigh's find
   Never that knew this suasive balm
That helps when Gilead's fails to heal,
   Helps by an interserted charm.

Insinuous thou that through the nerve
   Windest the soul, and so canst win
   Some from repinings, some from sin,
The Church's aim thou dost subserve.

The ruffled fag fordone with care
   And brooding, Gold would ease this pain:
Him soothest thou and smoothest down
Till some content return again.

Even ruffians feel thy influence breed
   Saint Martin's summer in the mind,
They feel this last evangel plead,
As did the first, apart from creed,
   Be peaceful, man – be kind!

V

Rejected once on higher plain,
O Love Supreme, to come again
   Can this be thine?

Again to come, and win us too
   In likeness of a weed
That as a god didst vainly woo,
   As man more vainly bleed?

VI

Forbear, my soul! and in thine Eastern chamber
   Rehearse the dream that brings the long release:
Through jasmine sweet and talismanic amber
   Inhaling Herba Santa in the passive Pipe of Peace.

HERMAN MELVILLE

Boeuf en Daube

An exquisite scent of olives and oil and juice rose from the great brown dish as Marthe, with a little flourish, took the cover off. The cook had spent three days over that dish. And she must take great care, Mrs Ramsay thought, diving into the soft mass, to choose a specially tender piece for William Bankes. And she peered into the dish, with its shiny walls and its confusion of savoury brown and yellow meats, and its bay leaves and its wine, and thought, This will celebrate the occasion – a curious sense rising in her, at once freakish and tender, of celebrating a festival, as if two emotions were called up in her, one profound – for what could be more serious than the love of man for woman, what more commanding, more impressive, bearing in its bosom the seeds of death; at the same time these lovers, these people entering into illusion glittering-eyed, must be danced round with mockery, decorated with garlands.

'It is a triumph,' said Mr Bankes, laying his knife down for a moment. He had eaten attentively. It was rich; it was tender. It was perfectly cooked. How did she manage these things in the depths of the country? he asked her. She was a wonderful woman. All his love, all his reverence had returned; and she knew it.

'It is a French recipe of my grandmother's,' said Mrs Ramsay, speaking with a ring of great pleasure in her voice. Of course it was French. What passes for cookery in England is an abomination (they agreed). It is putting cabbages in water. It is roasting meat till it is like leather. It is cutting off the delicious skins of vegetables. 'In which', said Mr Bankes, 'all the virtue of the vegetable is contained.' And the waste, said Mrs Ramsay. A whole French family could live on what an English cook throws away.

VIRGINIA WOOLF
from *To the Lighthouse*

Omelette aux tomates

It was on this pleasant basis of costly disorder, consequently, that they eventually seated themselves, on either side of a small table, at a window adjusted to the busy quay and the shining barge-burdened Seine; where, for an hour, in the matter of letting himself go, of diving deep, Strether was to feel he had touched bottom. He was to feel many things on this occasion, and one of the first of them was that he had travelled far since that evening in London, before the theatre, when his dinner with Maria Gostrey, between the pink-shaded candles, had struck him as requiring so many explanations. He had at that time gathered them in, the explanations – he had stored them up; but it was at present as if he had either soared above or sunk below them – he could n't tell which; he could somehow think of none that did n't seem to leave the appearance of collapse and cynicism easier for him than lucidity. How could he wish it to be lucid for others, for any one, that he, for the hour, saw reasons enough in the mere way the bright clean ordered water-side life came in at the open window? – the mere way Madame de Vionnet, opposite him over their intensely white table-linen, their *omelette aux tomates*, their bottle of straw-coloured Chablis, thanked him for everything almost with the smile of a child, while her grey eyes moved in and out of their talk, back to the quarter of the warm spring air, in which early summer had already begun to throb, and then back again to his face and their human questions.

HENRY JAMES
from *The Ambassadors*

A Peasant Supper

A shoe coming loose from the fore-foot of the thill-horse, at the beginning of the ascent of mount Taurira, the postillion dismounted, twisted the shoe off, and put it in his pocket; as the ascent was of five or six miles, and that horse our main dependence, I made a point of having the shoe fastened on again, as well as we could; but the postillion had thrown away the nails, and the hammer in the chaise-box being of no great use without them, I submitted to go on.

He had not mounted half a mile higher, when coming to a flinty piece of road, the poor devil lost a second shoe, and from off his other fore-foot; I then got out of the chaise in good earnest; and seeing a house about a quarter of a mile to the left-hand, with a great deal to do I prevailed upon the postillion to turn up to it. The look of the house, and of everything about it, as we drew nearer, soon reconciled me to the disaster. – It was a little farmhouse surrounded with about twenty acres of vineyard, about as much corn – and close to the house, on one side, was a *potagerie* of an acre and a half, full of everything which could make plenty in a French peasant's house – and on the other side was a little wood which furnished wherewithal to dress it. It was about eight in the evening when I got to the house – so I left the postillion to manage his point as he could – and for mine, I walked directly into the house.

The family consisted of an old grey-headed man and his wife, with five or six sons and sons-in-law, and their several wives, and a joyous genealogy out of 'em.

They were all sitting down together to their lentil-soup; a large wheaten loaf was in the middle of the table; and a flaggon of wine at each end of it promised joy through the stages of the repast – 'twas a feast of love.

The old man rose up to meet me, and with a respectful cordiality would have me sit down at the table; my heart was sat down the moment I entered the room; so I sat down at once like a son of the family; and to invest myself in the character as speedily as I could, I instantly borrowed the old man's knife, and taking up the loaf, cut myself a hearty luncheon; and as I did it, I saw a testimony in every eye, not only of an honest welcome, but of a welcome mixed with thanks that I had not seemed to doubt it.

Was it this; or tell me, Nature, what else it was which made this morsel so sweet – and to what magic I owe it, that the draught I took of their flaggon was so delicious with it, that they remain upon my palate to this hour?

LAURENCE STERNE
from *A Sentimental Journey*

Scrooge Observes the Cratchit Christmas

Such a bustle ensued that you might have thought a goose the rarest of all birds; a feathered phenomenon, to which a black swan was a matter of course; and in truth it was something very like it in that house. Mrs Cratchit made the gravy (ready beforehand in a little saucepan) hissing hot; Master Peter mashed the potatoes with incredible vigour; Miss Belinda sweetened up the apple-sauce; Martha dusted the hot plates; Bob took Tiny Tim beside him in a tiny corner at the table; the two young Cratchits set chairs for everybody, not forgetting themselves, and mounting guard upon their posts, crammed spoons into their mouths, lest they should shriek for goose before their turn came to be helped. At last the dishes were set on, and grace was said. It was succeeded by a breathless pause, as Mrs Cratchit, looking slowly all along the carving-knife, prepared to plunge it in the breast; but when she did, and when the long expected gush of stuffing issued forth, one murmur of delight arose all round the board, and even Tiny Tim, excited by the two young Cratchits, beat on the table with the handle of his knife, and feebly cried Hurrah!

There never was such a goose. Bob said he didn't believe there ever was such a goose cooked. Its tenderness and flavour, size and cheapness, were the themes of universal admiration. Eked out by the apple-sauce and mashed potatoes, it was a sufficient dinner for the whole family; indeed, as Mrs Cratchit said with great delight (surveying one small atom of a bone upon the dish), they hadn't ate it all at last! Yet every one had had enough, and the youngest Cratchits in particular, were steeped in sage and onion to the eyebrows! But now, the plates being changed by Miss Belinda, Mrs Cratchit left the room alone – too nervous to bear witnesses – to take the pudding up, and bring it in.

Suppose it should not be done enough! Suppose it should break in turning out! Suppose somebody should have got over the wall of the back-yard, and stolen it, while they were merry with the goose: a supposition at which the two young Cratchits became livid! All sorts of horrors were supposed.

Hallo! A great deal of steam! The pudding was out of the copper. A smell like a washing-day! That was the cloth. A smell like an eating-house, and a pastry-cook's next door to each other, with a laundress's next door to that! That was the pudding. In half a minute Mrs Cratchit entered: flushed, but smiling proudly: with the pudding, like a speckled cannon-ball, so hard and firm, blazing in half of half-a-quartern of ignited brandy, and bedight with Christmas holly stuck into the top.

Oh, a wonderful pudding! Bob Cratchit said, and calmly too, that he regarded it as the greatest success achieved by Mrs Cratchit since their marriage. Mrs Cratchit said that now the weight was off her mind, she would confess she had had her doubts about the quantity of flour. Everybody had something to say about it, but nobody said or thought it was at all a small pudding for a large family. It would have been flat heresy to do so. Any Cratchit would have blushed to hint at such a thing.

At last the dinner was all done, the cloth was cleared, the hearth swept, and the fire made up. The compound in the jug being tasted, and considered perfect, apples and oranges were put upon the table, and a shovel-full of chestnuts on the fire. Then all the Cratchit family drew round the hearth, in what Bob Cratchit called a circle, meaning half a one; and at Bob Cratchit's elbow stood the family display of glass; two tumblers, and a custard-cup without a handle.

These held the hot stuff from the jug, however, as well as golden goblets would have done; and Bob served it out with beaming looks, while the chestnuts on the fire sputtered and crackled noisily. Then Bob proposed:

'A Merry Christmas to us all, my dears. God bless us!'

Which all the family re-echoed.

'God bless us every one!' said Tiny Tim, the last of all.

He sat very close to his father's side, upon his little stool. Bob held his withered little hand in his, as if he loved the child, and wished to keep him by his side, and dreaded that he might be taken from him.

'Spirit,' said Scrooge, with an interest he had never felt before, 'tell me if Tiny Tim will live.'

CHARLES DICKENS
from *A Christmas Carol*

'That Phœbus *in his lofty race*'

That *Phœbus* in his lofty race,
Oft layes aside his beames
And comes to coole his glowing face
In these delicious streames;

Oft spreading Vines clime up the Cleeves,
Whose ripned clusters there,
Their liquid purple drop, which drives
A Vintage through thee yeere.

Those Cleeves whose craggy sides are clad
With Trees of sundry sutes,
Which make continuall summer glad,
Even bending with their fruits,

Some ripening, ready some to fall,
Some blossom'd, some to bloome,
Like gorgeous hangings on the wall
Of some rich princely Roome:

Pomegranates, *Lymons*, *Cytrons*, so
Their laded branches bow,
Their leaves in number that outgoe
Nor roomth will them alow.

There in perpetuall Summers shade,
Apolloes Prophets sit
Among the flowres that never fade,
But flowrish like their wit;

To whom the Nimphes upon their Lyres,
Tune many a curious lay,
And with their most melodious Quires
Make short the longest day.

MICHAEL DRAYTON

Priapus
Keeper-of-Orchards

I saw the first pear
as it fell—
the honey-seeking, golden-banded,
the yellow swarm
was not more fleet than I,
(spare us from loveliness)
and I fell prostrate,
crying.
you have flayed us
with thy blossoms,
spare us the beauty
of fruit-trees.

The honey-seeking
paused not,
the air thundered their song,
and I alone was prostrate.
O rough-hewn
god of the orchard,
I bring you an offering—
do you, alone unbeautiful,
son of the god,
spare us from loveliness:

these fallen hazel-nuts,
stripped late of their green sheaths,
grapes, red-purple,
their berries
dripping with wine,
pomegranates already broken,
and shrunken figs
and quinces untouched,
I bring you as offering.

H.D.

The Absinthe Drinker

Gently I wave the visible world away.
 Far off, I hear a roar, afar yet near,
 Far off and strange, a voice is in my ear,
And is the voice my own? the words I say
Fall strangely, like a dream, across the day;
 And the dim sunshine is a dream. How clear,
 New as the world to lovers' eyes, appear
The men and women passing on their way!

The world is very fair. The hours are all
   Linked in a dance of mere forgetfulness.
     I am at peace with God and man. O glide,
Sands of the hour-glass that I count not, fall
   Serenely: scarce I feel your soft caress,
     Rocked on this dreamy and indifferent tide.

ARTHUR SYMONS

A Dinner in Manhattan

'Oh George I'm starved, simply starved.'

'So am I' he said in a crackling voice. 'And Elaine I've got news for you,' he went on hurriedly as if he were afraid she'd interrupt him.

'Cecily has consented to a divorce. We're going to rush it through quietly in Paris this summer. Now what I want to know is, will you . . . ?'

She leaned over and patted his hand that grasped the edge of the table. 'George lets eat our dinner first . . . We've got to be sensible. God knows we've messed things up enough in the past both of us . . . Let's drink to the crime wave.' The smooth infinitesimal foam of the cocktail was soothing in her tongue and throat, glowed gradually warmly through her. She looked at him laughing with sparkling eyes. He drank his at a gulp.

'By gad Elaine,' he said flaming up helplessly, 'you're the most wonderful thing in the world.'

Through dinner she felt a gradual icy coldness stealing through her like novocaine. She had made up her mind. It seemed as if she had set the photograph of herself in her own place, forever frozen into a single gesture. An invisible silk band of bitterness was tightening round her throat, strangling. Beyond the plates, the ivory pink lamp, the broken pieces of bread, his face above the blank shirtfront jerked and nodded; the flush grew on his cheeks; his nose caught the light now on one side, now on the other, his taut lips moved eloquently over his yellow teeth. Ellen felt herself sitting with her ankles crossed, rigid as a porcelain figure under her clothes, everything about her seemed to be growing hard and enameled, the air bluestreaked with cigarettesmoke, was turning to glass.

JOHN DOS PASSOS
from *Manhattan Transfer*

The Three Sailors

There were three sailors in Bristol city,
Who took a boat and went to sea.

But first with beef and captain's biscuit,
And pickled pork they loaded she.

There was guzzling Jack and gorging Jimmy,
And the youngest he was little Bill-*ly*.

Now very soon they were so greedy,
They didn't leave not one split pea.

Says guzzling Jack to gorging Jimmy,
'I am confounded hung-*ery*.'

Says gorging Jim to guzzling Jacky,
'We have no wittles, so we must eat *we*.'

Says guzzling Jack to gorging Jimmy,
'Oh! gorging Jim, what a fool you be!'

'There's little Bill as is young and tender,
We're old and tough – so let's eat *he*.'

'Oh! Bill, we're going to kill and eat you,
So undo the collar of your chemie.'

When Bill he heard this information,
He used his pocket-handkerchie.

'Oh! let me say my catechism,
As my poor mammy taught to me.'

'Make haste, make haste,' says guzzling Jacky,
Whilst Jim pulled out his snicker-snee.

So Bill went up the maintop-gallant mast,
When down he fell on his bended knee.

He scarce had said his catechism,
When up he jumps; 'There's land I see:

'There's Jerusalem and Madagascar,
And North and South Ameri-*key*.

'There's the British fleet a-riding at anchor,
With Admiral Napier, K.C.B.'

So when they came to the Admiral's vessel,
He hanged fat Jack, and flogged Jim-*my*.

But as for little Bill, he made him
The Captain of a Seventy-three.

WILLIAM MAKEPEACE THACKERAY

Dinner in Lilliput

... being almost famished with hunger, having not eaten a morsel for some hours before I left the ship, I found the demands of nature so strong upon me, that I could not forbear showing my impatience (perhaps against the strict rules of decency) by putting my finger frequently on my mouth, to signify that I wanted food. The *Hurgo* (for so they call a great lord, as I afterwards learnt) understood me very well. He descended from the stage, and commanded that several ladders should be applied to my sides, on which above an hundred of the inhabitants mounted, and walked towards my mouth, laden with baskets full of meat, which had been provided and sent thither by the King's orders upon the first intelligence he received of me. I observed there was the flesh of several animals, but could not distinguish them by the taste. There were shoulders, legs and loins, shaped like those of mutton, and very well dressed, but smaller than the wings of a lark. I ate them by two or three at a mouthful, and took three loaves at a time, about the bigness of musket bullets. They supplied me as fast as they could, showing a thousand marks of wonder and astonishment at my bulk and appetite. I then made another sign that I wanted drink. They found by my eating that a small quantity would not suffice me; and being a most ingenious people, they slung up with great dexterity one of their largest hogsheads, then rolled it towards my hand, and beat out the top; I drank it off at a draught, which I might well do, for it hardly held half a pint, and tasted like a small wine of Burgundy, but much more delicious. They brought me a second hogshead, which I drank in the same manner, and made signs for more, but they had none to give me.

JONATHAN SWIFT
from *Gulliver's Travels*

Dinner in Brobdingnag

It was about twelve at noon, and a servant brought in dinner. It was only one substantial dish of meat (fit for the plain condition of an husbandman) in a dish of about four and twenty foot diameter. The company were the farmer and his wife, three children, and an old grandmother: when they were sat down, the farmer placed me at some distance from him on the table, which was thirty foot high from the floor. I was in a terrible fright, and kept as far as I could from the edge for fear of falling. The wife minced a bit of meat, then crumbled some bread on a trencher, and placed it before me. I made her a low bow, took out my knife and fork, and fell to eat, which gave them exceeding delight. The mistress sent her maid for a small dram-cup, which held about two gallons, and filled it with drink; I took up the vessel with much difficulty in both hands, and in a most respectful manner drank to her ladyship's health, expressing the words as loud as I could in English, which made the company laugh so heartily, that I was almost deafened with the noise. This liquor tasted like a small cider, and was not unpleasant. Then the master made me a sign to come to his trencher side; but as I walked on the table, being in great surprise all the time, as the indulgent reader will easily conceive and excuse, I happened to stumble against a crust, and fell flat on my face, but received no hurt.

JONATHAN SWIFT
from *Gulliver's Travels*

The Queen of Brobdingnag

The Queen became so fond of my company, that she could not dine without me. I had a table placed upon the same at which her Majesty ate, just at her left elbow, and a chair to sit on.

Glumdalclitch stood upon a stool on the floor, near my table, to assist and take care of me. I had an entire set of silver dishes and plates, and other necessaries, which, in proportion to those of the Queen, were not much bigger than what I have seen in a London toy-shop, for the furniture of a baby-house: these my little nurse kept in her pocket, in a silver box, and gave me at meals as I wanted them, always cleaning them herself. No person dined with the Queen but the two Princesses Royal, the elder sixteen years old, and the younger at that time thirteen and a month. Her Majesty used to put a bit of meat upon one of my dishes, out of which I carved for myself; and her diversion was to see me eat in miniature. For the Queen (who had indeed but a weak stomach) took up at one mouthful as much as a dozen English farmers could eat at a meal, which to me was for some time a very nauseous sight. She would craunch the wing of a lark, bones and all, between her teeth, although it were nine times as large as that of a full-grown turkey; and put a bit of bread in her mouth, as big as two twelve-penny loaves. She drank out of a golden cup, above a hogshead at a draught.

JONATHAN SWIFT
from *Gulliver's Travels*

Dinner in Houyhnhnms Land

When dinner was done, the master horse took me aside, and by signs and words made me understand the concern he was in, that I had nothing to eat. Oats in their tongue are called *blunnb*. This word I pronounced two or three times; for although I had refused them at first, yet upon second thoughts, I considered that I could contrive to make of them a kind of bread, which might be sufficient with milk to keep me alive, till I could make my escape to some other country, and to creatures of my own species. The horse immediately ordered a white mare-servant of his family to bring me a good quantity of oats in a sort of wooden tray. These I heated before the fire as well as I could, and rubbed them till the husks came off, which I made a shift to winnow from the grain; I ground and beat them between two stones, then took water, and made them into a paste or cake, which I toasted at the fire, and ate warm with milk. It was at first a very insipid diet, although common enough in many parts of Europe, but grew tolerable by time; and having been often reduced to hard fare in my life, this was not the first experiment I had made how easily nature is satisfied. And I cannot but observe, that I never had one hour's sickness, while I stayed in this island. 'Tis true, I sometimes made a shift to catch a rabbit, or bird, by springes made of Yahoos' hairs, and I often gathered wholesome herbs, which I boiled, or ate as salads with my bread, and now and then, for a rarity, I made a little butter, and drank the whey. I was at first at a great loss for salt; but custom soon reconciled the want of it; and I am confident that the frequent use of salt among us is an effect of luxury, and was first introduced only as a provocative to drink; except where it is necessary for preserving of flesh in long voyages, or in places remote from great markets. For we observe no animal to be fond of it but man: and as to myself, when I left this country, it was a great while before I could endure the taste of it in anything that I ate.

JONATHAN SWIFT
from *Gulliver's Travels*

Seamen Three

Seamen three! What men be ye?
Gotham's three wise men we be.
Whither in your bowl so free?
To rake the moon from out the sea.

The bowl goes trim. The moon doth shine.
And our ballast is old wine;
And your ballast is old wine.

Who art thou, so fast adrift?
I am he they call Old Care,
Here on board we will thee lift.
No: I may not enter there.
Wherefore so? 'Tis Jove's decree,
In a bowl Care may not be;
In a bowl Care may not be.

Fear ye not the waves that roll?
No: in charmed bowl we swim.
What the charm that floats the bowl?
Water may not pass the brim.
The bowl goes trim. The moon doth shine.
And our ballast is old wine;
And your ballast is old wine.

THOMAS LOVE PEACOCK

The Laird's Hospitality

The Laird of Milnwood kept up all old fashions which were connected with economy. It was, therefore, still the custom in his house, as it had been universal in Scotland about fifty years before, that the domestics, after having placed the dinner on the table, sate down at the lower end of the board, and partook of the share which was assigned to them, in company with their masters. Upon the day, therefore, after Cuddie's arrival, being the third from the opening of this narrative, old Robin, who was butler, valet-de-chambre, footman, gardener, and what not, in the house of Milnwood, placed on the table an immense charger of broth, thickened with oatmeal and colewort, in which ocean of liquid were indistinctly discovered, by close observers, two or three short ribs of lean mutton sailing to and fro. Two huge baskets, one of bread made of barley and pease, and one of oatcakes, flanked this standing dish. A large boiled salmon would now-a-days have indicated more liberal house-keeping; but at that period that fish was caught in such plenty in the considerable rivers in Scotland, that instead of being accounted a delicacy, it was generally applied to feed the servants, who are said sometimes to have stipulated that they should not be required to eat a food so luscious and surfeiting in its quality above five times a-week. The large black jack, filled with very small beer of Milnwood's own brewing, was indulged to the company at discretion, as were the bannocks, cakes, and broth; but the mutton was reserved for the heads of the family, Mrs Wilson included: and a measure of ale, somewhat deserving the name, was set apart in a silver tankard for their exclusive use. A huge kebbock (a cheese, that is, made with ewe-milk mixed with cow's milk) and a jar of salt butter, were in common to the company.

To enjoy this exquisite cheer, was placed, at the head of the table, the old Laird himself, with his nephew on the one side, and the favourite housekeeper on the other. At a long interval, and beneath the salt of course, sate old Robin, a meagre, half-starved serving-man, rendered cross and cripple by the rheumatism, and a dirty drab of a housemaid, whom use had rendered callous to the daily exercitations which her temper underwent at the hands of her master and Mrs Wilson. A barnman, a white-headed cow-herd boy, with Cuddie the new ploughman and his mother, completed the party. The other labourers belonging to the property resided in their own houses, happy at least in this, that if their cheer was not more delicate than that which we have described, they could at least eat their fill, unwatched by the sharp, envious grey eyes of Milnwood, which seemed to measure the quantity that each of his dependents swallowed, as closely as if their glances attended each mouthful in its progress from the lips to the stomach. This close inspection was unfavourable to Cuddie, who sustained much prejudice in his new master's opinion, by the silent celerity with which he caused the victuals to disappear before him. And ever and anon Milnwood turned his eyes from the huge feeder to cast indignant glances upon his nephew, whose repugnance to rustic labour was the principal cause of his needing a ploughman, and who had been the direct means of his hiring this very cormorant.

'Pay thee wages, quotha?' said Milnwood to himself – 'Thou wilt eat in a week the value of mair than thou canst work for in a month.'

SIR WALTER SCOTT
from *Old Mortality*

Lines Inscribed upon a Cup Formed from a Skull

Start not – nor deem my spirit fled;
  In me behold the only skull,
From which, unlike a living head,
  Whatever flows is never dull.

I lived, I loved, I quaff'd, like thee:
  I died: let earth my bones resign;
Fill up – thou canst not injure me;
  The worm hath fouler lips than thine.

Better to hold the sparkling grape,
  That nurse the earth-worm's slimy brood;
And circle in the goblet's shape
  The drink of gods, than reptile's food.

Where once my wit, perchance, hath shone,
    In aid of others' let me shine;
And when, alas! our brains are gone,
    What nobler substitute than wine?

Quaff while thou canst: another race,
    When thou and thine, like me, are sped,
May rescue thee from earth's embrace,
    And rhyme and revel with the dead.

Why not? since through life's little day
    Our heads such sad effects produce;
Redeem'd from worms and wasting clay,
    This chance is theirs, to be of use.

LORD BYRON

'Desire of wine and all delicious drinks'

Desire of wine and all delicious drinks,
Which many a famous warrior overturns,
Thou could'st repress; nor did the dancing ruby,
Sparkling, out-poured, the flavour, or the smell,
Or taste that cheers the hearts of gods and men,
Allure thee from the cool crystálline stream.

JOHN MILTON
from *Samson Agonistes*

'And lately, by the Tavern Door agape'

And lately, by the Tavern Door agape,
Came stealing through the Dusk an Angel Shape
   Bearing a Vessel on his Shoulder; and
He bid me taste of it; and 'twas – the Grape!

The Grape that can with Logic absolute
The Two-and-Seventy jarring Sects confute:
   The subtle Alchemist that in a Trice
Life's leaden Metal into Gold transmute.

EDWARD FITZGERALD
from *The Rubáiyát of Omar Khayyám*

The Misers' Wedding Breakfast

Mr and Mrs Henry Earlforward, who were alone and rather
self-conscious and rather at a loss for something to do in the
beautiful shut shop, heard steps on the upper stairs. Elsie! They
had forgotten Elsie! It was not a time for them to be thoughtful
of other people. Elsie presently appeared on the lower stairs,
and was beheld of both her astonished employers. For Elsie was
clothed in her best, and it was proved that she indeed had a
best. Neither Henry nor Violet had ever seen the frock which
Elsie was wearing. Yet it was obviously not a new frock. It had
lain in that tin trunk of hers since more glorious days. Possibly
Joe might have seen it on some bright evening, but no other
among living men. Its colour was brown; in cut it did not bear,
and never had borne, any relation to the fashions of the day.
But it was unquestionably a best dress. Over the façade of the
front Elsie displayed a garment still more surprising; namely, a

white apron. Now in Clerkenwell white aprons were white only once in their active careers, and not always even once. White aprons in Clerkenwell were white (unless bought 'shop-soiled' at a reduction) for about the first hour of their first wearing. They were, of course, washed, rinsed and ironed, and sometimes lightly starched, but they never achieved whiteness again, and it was impossible that they should do so. A whitish grey was the highest they could reach after the first laundry. Elsie therefore was wearing a new apron; and, in fact, she had purchased it with her own money under the influence of her modest pride in forming a regular part of a household comprising a gentleman and lady freshly united in matrimony. She had also purchased a cap, but at the last moment, after trying it on, had lacked the courage to keep it on; she felt too excessively odd in it. She was carrying a parcel in her left hand, and the other was behind her back. Mrs Earlforward, at sight of her, guessed part of what was coming, but not the more exciting part.

'Oh, Elsie!' cried Mrs Earlforward. 'There you are! I fancied you were out.'

'No, 'm,' said Elsie, in her gentle, firm voice. 'But I wasn't expecting you and master home so early, and as soon as you came I run upstairs to change.'

With that Elsie, from the advantage of three stairs, suddenly showed her right hand, and out of a paper bag flung a considerable quantity of rice on to the middle-aged persons of the married. She accomplished this gesture with the air of a benevolent priestess performing a necessary and gravely important rite. Some of the rice stuck on its targets, but most of it rattled on the floor and rolled about in the silence. Indeed, there was quite a mess of rice on the floor, and the pity seemed to be that the vacuum-cleaners had left early.

Violet was the first to recover from the state of foolish and abashed stupefaction into which the deliberate assault had put man and wife. Violet laughed heartily, very heartily. Her mood was transformed again in an instant into one of gaiety, happiness, and natural ease. It was as if a sinister spell had been miraculously lifted. Henry gradually smiled, while regarding with proper regret this wanton waste of a health-giving food such as formed the sole nourishment of many millions of his fellow-creatures in distant parts of the world. Sheepishly brushing his clothes with his hand, he felt as though he was dissipating good rice-puddings. But he, too, suffered a change of heart.

'I had to do it, because it's for luck,' Elsie amiably explained, not without dignity. Evidently she had determined to do the wedding thoroughly, in spite of the unconventionalities of the contracting parties.

'I'm sure it's very kind of you,' said Mrs Earlforward.

'Yes, it is,' Mr Earlforward concurred.

'And here's a present from me,' Elsie continued, blushing, and offering the parcel.

'I'm sure we're very much obliged,' said Mrs Earlforward, taking the parcel. 'Come into the back-room, Elsie, and I'll undo it. It's very heavy. No, I'd better not hold it by the string.'

And in the office the cutting of string and the unfolding of brown paper and of tissue paper disclosed a box, and the opening of the box disclosed a wedding-cake – not a large one, true, but authentic. What with the shoe and the rice and the cake, Elsie in the grand generosity of her soul must have spent a fortune on the wedding, must have exercised the large munificence of a Rothschild – and all because she had faith in the virtue of the ancient proprieties appertaining to the marriage ceremony. She alone had seen Mrs Earlforward as a bride and Mr Earlforward as a bridegroom, and the magic of her belief compelled the partners also to see themselves as bride and bridegroom.

'Well, Elsie,' Violet burst out – and she was deeply affected – 'I really don't know what to say. It's most unexpected, and I don't know how to thank you. But run and get a knife, and we'll cut it.'

'It must be cut,' said Elsie, again the priestess, and she obedi-
ently ran off to get the knife.

'Well, well! . . . Well, well!' murmured Henry, flabbergasted,
and blushing even more than his wife had blushed. The pair
were so disturbed that they dared not look at each other.

'You must cut it, 'm,' said Elsie, returning with the knife and
a flat dish.

And Mrs Earlforward, having placed the cake on the dish,
sawed down into the cake. She had to use all her strength to
penetrate the brown; the top icing splintered easily, and frag-
ments of it flew about the desk.

'Now, Elsie, here's your slice,' said Violet, lifting the dish.

'Thank ye, 'm. But I must keep mine. I've got a little box for
it upstairs.'

'But aren't you going to eat any of it?'

'No, 'm,' with solemnity. 'But *you* must . . . I'll just taste this
white part,' she added, picking up a bit of icing from the desk.

The married pair ate.

'I think I'll go now, 'm, if you'll excuse me,' said Elsie. 'But
I'll just sweep up in the shop here first.' She was standing in
the doorway.

They heard her with hand-brush and dustpan collecting the
scattered food of the Orient. She peeped in at the door again.

'Good night, 'm. Good night, sir.' She saluted them with
a benignant grin in which was a surprising little touch of
naughtiness. And then they heard her receding footfalls as she
ascended cautiously the dark flights of stairs and entered into
her inviolable private life on the top floor.

'It would never have done not to eat it,' said Violet.

'No,' Henry agreed.

'She's a wonder, that girl is! You could have knocked me
down with a feather.'

'Yes.'

'I wonder where she bought it.'

'Must have gone up to King's Cross. Or down to Holborn. King's Cross more likely. Yesterday. In her dinner-hour.'

'I'm hungry,' said Violet.

And it was a fact that they had had no evening meal, seeing that they had expressly announced their intention of 'eating out' on that great day.

'So must you be, my dear,' said Violet.

There they were, alone together on the ground-floor, with one electric bulb in the back-room and one other, needlessly, lighting the middle part of the cleansed and pleasant shop. They could afford to be young and to live perilously, madly, absurdly. They lost control of themselves, and gloried in so doing. The cake was a danger to existence. It had the consistency of marble, the richness of molasses, the mysteriousness of the enigma of the universe. It seemed unconquerable. It seemed more fatal than daggers or gelignite. But they attacked it. Fortunately, neither of them knew the inner meaning of indigestion. When Henry had taken the last slice, Violet exclaimed like a child:

'Oh, just one tiny piece more!' And with burning eyes she bent down and bit off a morsel from the slice in Henry's hand.

'I am living!' shouted an unheard voice in Henry's soul.

ARNOLD BENNETT
from *Riceyman Steps*

Inuiting a Friend to Supper

To night, graue sir, both my poore house, and I
    Doe equally desire your companie:
Not that we thinke vs worthy such a ghest,
    But that your worth will dignifie our feast,
With those that come; whose grace may make that seeme
    Something, which, else, could hope for no esteeme.

It is the faire acceptance, Sir, creates
    The entertaynment perfect: not the cates.
Yet shall you haue, to rectifie your palate,
    An oliue, capers, or some better sallade
Vshring the mutton; with a short-leg'd hen,
    If we can get her, full of egs, and then,
Limons, and wine for sauce: to these, a coney
    Is not to be despair'd of, for our money;
And, though fowle, now, be scarce, yet there are clarkes,
    The skie not falling, thinke we may haue larkes.
Ile tell you of more, and lye, so you will come:
    Of patrich, pheasant, wood-cock, of which some
May yet be there; and godwit, if we can:
    Knat, raile, and ruffe too. How so ere, my man
Shall reade a piece of VIRGIL, TACITVS,
    LIVIE, or of some better booke to vs,
Of which wee'll speake our minds, amidst our meate;
    And Ill professe no verses to repeate:
To this, if ought appeare, which I know not of,
    That will the pastrie, not my paper, show of.
Digestiue cheese, and fruit there sure will bee;
    But that, which most doth take my *Muse*, and mee,
Is a pure cup of rich *Canary*-wine,
    Which is the *Mermaids*, now, but shall be mine:
Of which had HORACE, or ANACREON tasted,
    Their liues, as doe their lines, till now had lasted.
Tabacco, *Nectar*, or the *Thespian* spring,
    Are all but LUTHERS beere, to this I sing.
Of this we will sup free, but moderately,
    And we will haue no *Pooly'*, or *Parrot* by;
Nor shall our cups make any guiltie men:
    But, at our parting, we will be, as when

We innocently met. No simple word,
    That shall be vtter'd at our mirthfull boord,
Shall make vs sad next morning: or affright
    The libertie, that wee'll enjoy to night.

BEN JONSON

Turtle, Lobsters and Punch

It is impossible for me to explain how it was that she and I never married. We two knew exceedingly well, and that must suffice for the reader. There was the most perfect sympathy and understanding between us; we knew that neither of us would marry anyone else. I had asked her to marry me a dozen times over; having said this much I will say no more upon a point which is in no way necessary for the development of my story. For the last few years there had been difficulties in the way of our meeting, and I had not seen her, though, as I have said, keeping up a close correspondence with her. Naturally I was overjoyed to meet her again; she was now just thirty years old, but I thought she looked handsomer than ever.

Her father, of course, was the lion of the party, but seeing that we were all meek and quite willing to be eaten, he roared to us rather than at us. It was a fine sight to see him tucking his napkin under his rosy old gills, and letting it fall over his capacious waistcoat while the high light from the chandelier danced about the bump of benevolence on his bald old head like a star of Bethlehem.

The soup was real turtle; the old gentleman was evidently well pleased and he was beginning to come out. Gelstrap stood behind his master's chair. I sat next Mrs Theobald on her left hand, and was thus just opposite her father-in-law, whom I had every opportunity of observing.

During the first ten minutes or so, which were taken up with the soup and the bringing of the fish, I should probably have thought, if I had not long since made up my mind about him, what a fine old man he was and how proud his children should be of him; but suddenly as he was helping himself to lobster sauce, he flushed crimson, a look of extreme vexation suffused his face, and he darted two furtive but fiery glances to the two ends of the table, one for Theobald and one for Christina. They, poor simple souls, of course, saw that something was exceedingly wrong, and so did I, but I couldn't guess what it was till I heard the old man hiss in Christina's ear: 'It was not made with a hen lobster. What's the use,' he continued, 'of my calling the boy Ernest, and getting him christened in water from the Jordan, if his own father does not know a cock from a hen lobster?'

This cut me too, for I felt that till that moment I had not so much as known that there were cocks and hens among lobsters, but had vaguely thought that in the matter of matrimony they were even as the angels in heaven, and grew up almost spontaneously from rocks and seaweed.

Before the next course was over Mr Pontifex had recovered his temper, and from that time to the end of the evening he was at his best. He told us all about the water from the Jordan; how it had been brought by Dr Jones along with some stone jars of water from the Rhine, the Rhone, the Elbe and the Danube, and what trouble he had had with them at the Custom Houses, and how the intention had been to make punch with waters from all the greatest rivers in Europe; and how he, Mr Pontifex, had saved the Jordan water from going into the bowl, etc., etc. 'No, no, no,' he continued, 'it wouldn't have done at all, you know; very profane idea; so we each took a pint bottle of it home with us, and the punch was much better without it.

I had a narrow escape with mine, though, the other day; I fell over a hamper in the cellar, when I was getting it up to bring to Battersby, and if I had not taken the greatest care the bottle would certainly have been broken, but I saved it.' And Gelstrap was standing behind the chair all the time!

Nothing more happened to ruffle Mr Pontifex, so we had a delightful evening, which has often recurred to me while watching the after career of my godson.

SAMUEL BUTLER
from *The Way of All Flesh*

'Faustinus is a man of taste'

Faustinus is a man of taste;
Yet is his Baian seat no waste
Of useless myrtle, barren plane,
Clipped box, like many a grand domain
That covers miles with empty state:
But country unsophisticate.
In every corner grain is crammed,
Casks fragrant of old wine are jammed.
Here, at the turning of the year,
Vinedressers house the vintage sere.
Grim bulls in grassy valleys low
And the calf butts with hornless brow.
Poultry of every clime and sort
Ramble in dirt about the court,
The screaming geese, flamingoes red,
Peacocks with jewelled tail outspread,
Pied partridges, pheasants that come
From Colchian strand, dark magic's home,
And Afric's birds of many spots.
The cock amidst his harem struts

While on the tower aloft doves coo
And pigeons flap and turtles woo.
Pigs to the good wife's apron scurry,
Lambs to their milky mothers hurry.
The fire, well-heaped, burns bright and high,
Around it crowds the nursery.
No butler here from lack of toil
Grows sick, no trainer wastes his oil,
Lounging at ease; but forth they fare
The fish with quivering line to snare,
The crafty springe for birds to set,
Or catch the deer with circling net.
Pleased with the garden's easy work
The city hands take spade and fork;
The curly-headed striplings ask
The bailiff for a merry task
Without their pedagogue's command;
E'en the sleek eunuch bears a hand.
Then country callers, many a one,
Troop in, and empty-handed none;
This brings a honeycomb, that a pail
Of milk from green Sassinum's dale;
Capons or dormice plump another,
Or kid, reft from his shaggy mother.
Basket on arm, stout lasses come
With gifts from many a thrifty home.
Work over, each, a willing guest,
Is bidden to no niggard feast,
Where all may revel at their will,
And servants eat, like guests, their fill.
But thou, friend Bassus, close to town,
On trim starvation lookest down,
Seest laurels, laurels everywhere;
No need the thief from fruit to scare.

Town bread thy vinedresser must eat;
The town sends greens, eggs, cheese, and meat.
Such country is – my friend must own –
Not country, but town out of town.

GOLDWIN SMITH

On the Guyana–Brazil Border

The chief man of the place offered me formal hospitality in the shape of *cassiri* in a tin bowl of European manufacture. I put it to my lips and passed it on to Eusebio. *Cassiri* is the drink of the country from time immemorial. (It is curious how propagandists always talk as though alcohol had been introduced to the backward races by principled traders and imperialists, referring ironically to the joint import of gin and hymn books. In point of fact almost every race had discovered it for themselves centuries before European explorers appeared on the scene at all and used it on a large scale for frequent, prolonged orgies, besides which the most ambitious American parties appear austerely temperate.) It is made from sweet cassava roots, chewed up by the elder members of the community and spat into a bowl. The saliva starts fermentation, and the result is a thick, pinkish liquor of mildly intoxicating property. I was a little sceptical about the orgiastic nature of the ceremonial *cassiri* parties until I saw the vat in which it is kept. There is one or more in every village, according to its size. There were two at Karasabai in the back of the hut where we were quartered, and I took them at first to be boats, for they consisted – like most of the craft on those rivers – of entire tree trunks hollowed out. Before a party – and Father Keary told me with regret that the tendency was for the parties to become more frequent – the whole village chews and spits indefatigably until the vat or vats are completely full. Then, after the fermentation has been under way for some time, they all assemble and drink the entire quantity. It usually takes some days, beginning sombrely like all Indian functions, warming up to dancing and courtship and ending with the whole village insensibly drunk.

EVELYN WAUGH
from *Ninety-Two Days*

'But if to ease his busy breast'

But if to ease his busy breast
He thinks of *home*, and taking rest,
A *rural cot*, and *common fare*
Are all his *cordials* against *care*.
There at the *door* of his low *cell*
Under some *shade*, or near some *well*
Where the *cool poplar* grows, his *plate*
Of common *earth*, without more *state*
Expect their *lord*. *Salt* in a *shell*,
Green *cheese*, thin *beer*, *draughts* that will *tell*
No *tales*, a *hospitable cup*,
With some *fresh berries* do make up
His healthful feast, nor doth he wish
For the fat *carp*, or a rare dish
Of *Lucrine oysters*; the swift *quist*
Or *pigeon* sometimes (if he list)
With the *slow goose* that loves the *stream*,
Fresh, various *salads*, and the *bean*

By curious *palates* never sought,
And to close with, some cheap unbought
Dish for *digestion*, are the most
And choicest *dainties* he can *boast*.

HENRY VAUGHAN

Circe awaits Ulysses' Ship

Oh, look! a speck on this side of the sun,
Coming – yes, coming with the rising wind
That frays the darkening cloud-wrack on the verge
And in a little while will leap abroad,
Spattering the sky with rushing blacknesses,
Dashing the hissing mountainous waves at the stars.
'Twill drive me that black speck a shuddering hulk
Caught in the buffeting waves, dashed impotent
From ridge to ridge, will drive it in the night
With that dull jarring crash upon the beach,
And the cries for help and the cries of fear and hope.
    And then to-morrow they will thoughtfully,
With grave low voices, count their perils up,
And thank the gods for having let them live,
And tell of wives or mothers in their homes,
And children, who would have such loss in them
That they must weep (and may be I weep too)
With fancy of the weepings had they died.
And the next morrow they will feel their ease
And sigh with sleek content, or laugh elate,
Tasting delights of rest and revelling,
Music and perfumes, joyaunce for the eyes
Of rosy faces and luxurious pomps,
The savour of the banquet and the glow

And fragrance of the wine-cup; and they'll talk
How good it is to house in palaces
Out of the storms and struggles, and what luck
Strewed their good ship on our accessless coast.
Then the next day the beast in them will wake,
And one will strike and bicker, and one swell
With puffed up greatness, and one gibe and strut
In apish pranks, and one will line his sleeve
With pilfered booties, and one snatch the gems
Out of the carven goblets as they pass,
One will grow mad with fever of the wine,
And one will sluggishly besot himself,
And one be lewd, and one be gluttonous;
And I shall sickly look, and loathe them all.

Oh my rare cup! my pure and crystal cup
With not one speck of colour to make false
The entering lights, or flaw to make them swerve!
My cup of Truth! How the lost fools will laugh
And thank me for my boon, as if I gave
Some momentary flash of the gods' joy,
To drink where *I* have drunk and touch the touch
Of *my* lips with their own! Aye, let them touch.
Too cruel am I? And the silly beasts,
Crowding around me when I pass their way,
Glower on me and, although they love me still,
(With their poor sorts of love such as they could)
Call wrath and vengeance to their humid eyes
To scare me into mercy, or creep near
With piteous fawnings, supplicating bleats.
Too cruel? Did I choose them what they are?
Or change them from themselves by poisonous charms?
But any draught, pure water, natural wine,
Out of my cup, revealed them to themselves

And to each other. Change? there was no change;
Only disguise gone from them unawares:
And had there been one true right man of them
He would have drunk the draught as I had drunk,
And stood unharmed and looked me in the eyes,
Abashing me before him. But these things –
Why, which of them has even shown the kind
Of some one nobler beast? Pah! yapping wolves
And pitiless stealthy wild-cats, curs and apes
And gorging swine and slinking venomous snakes,
All false and ravenous and sensual brutes
That shame the Earth that bore them, these they are.

Lo, lo! the shivering blueness darting forth
On half the heaven, and the forked thin fire
Strikes to the sea, and hark, the sudden voice
That rushes through the trees before the storm,
And shuddering of the branches. Yet the sky
Is blue against them still, and early stars
Sparkle above the pine-tops; and the air
Clings faint and motionless around me here.

Another burst of flame – and the black speck
Shows in the glare, lashed onwards. It were well
I bade make ready for our guests to-night.

AUGUSTA WEBSTER

A Dinner in Italy

Philip discerned in the corner behind her a young man who
might eventually prove handsome and well-made, but certainly
did not seem so then. He was half enveloped in the drapery of

a cold dirty curtain, and nervously stuck out a hand, which Philip took and found thick and damp. There were more murmurs of approval from the stairs.

'Well, din-din's nearly ready,' said Lilia. 'Your room's down the passage, Philip. You needn't go changing.'

He stumbled away to wash his hands, utterly crushed by her effrontery.

'Dear Caroline!' whispered Lilia as soon as he had gone. 'What an angel you've been to tell him! He takes it so well. But you must have had a *mauvais quart d'heure.*'

Miss Abbott's long terror suddenly turned into acidity. 'I've told nothing,' she snapped. 'It's all for you – and if it only takes a quarter of an hour you'll be lucky!'

Dinner was a nightmare. They had the smelly dining-room to themselves. Lilia, very smart and vociferous, was at the head of the table; Miss Abbott, also in her best, sat by Philip, looking, to his irritated nerves, more like the tragedy confidante every moment. That scion of the Italian nobility, Signor Carella, sat opposite. Behind him loomed a bowl of goldfish, who swam round and round, gaping at the guests.

The face of Signor Carella was twitching too much for Philip to study it. But he could see the hands, which were not particularly clean, and did not get cleaner by fidgeting amongst the shining slabs of hair. His starched cuffs were not clean either, and as for his suit, it had obviously been bought for the occasion as something really English – a gigantic check, which did not even fit. His handkerchief he had forgotten, but never missed it. Altogether, he was quite unpresentable, and very lucky to have a father who was a dentist in Monteriano. And why even Lilia – but as soon as the meal began it furnished Philip with an explanation.

For the youth was hungry, and his lady filled his plate with spaghetti, and when those delicious slippery worms were flying down his throat his face relaxed and became for a moment unconscious and calm. And Philip had seen that face before in Italy a hundred times – seen it and loved it, for it was not merely beautiful, but had the charm which is the rightful heritage of all who are born on that soil. But he did not want to see it opposite him at dinner. It was not the face of a gentleman.

Conversation, to give it that name, was carried on in a mixture of English and Italian. Lilia had picked up hardly any of the latter language, and Signor Carella had not yet learned any of the former. Occasionally Miss Abbott had to act as interpreter between the lovers, and the situation became uncouth and revolting in the extreme. Yet Philip was too cowardly to break forth and denounce the engagement. He thought he should be more effective with Lilia if he had her alone, and pretended to himself that he must hear her defence before giving judgement.

Signor Carella, heartened by the spaghetti and the throat-rasping wine, attempted to talk, and, looking politely towards Philip, said: 'England is a great country. The Italians love England and the English.'

Philip, in no mood for international amenities, merely bowed.

'Italy too,' the other continued a little resentfully, 'is a great country. She has produced many famous men – for example, Garibaldi and Dante. The latter wrote the *Inferno*, the *Purgatorio*, the *Paradiso*. The *Inferno* is the most beautiful.' And, with the complacent tone of one who has received a solid education, he quoted the opening lines –

> Nel mezzo del cammin di nostra vita
> Mi ritrovai per una selva oscura,
> Che la diritta via era smarrita –

a quotation which was more apt than he supposed.

Lilia glanced at Philip to see whether he noticed that she was marrying no ignoramus. Anxious to exhibit all the good qualities of her betrothed, she abruptly introduced the subject of *pallone*,

in which, it appeared, he was a proficient player. He suddenly
became shy, and developed a conceited grin – the grin of the
village yokel whose cricket score is mentioned before a stranger.
Philip himself had loved to watch *pallone*, that entrancing combination of lawn-tennis and fives. But he did not expect to
love it quite so much again.

'Oh, look!' exclaimed Lilia, 'the poor wee fish!'

A starved cat had been worrying them all for pieces of the
purple quivering beef they were trying to swallow. Signor Carella,
with the brutality so common in Italians, had caught her by the
paw and flung her away from him. Now she had climbed up to
the bowl and was trying to hook out the fish. He got up, drove
her off, and, finding a large glass stopper by the bowl, entirely
plugged up the aperture with it.

'But may not the fish die?' said Miss Abbott. 'They have no
air.'

'Fish live on water, not on air,' he replied in a knowing voice,
and sat down. Apparently he was at his ease again, for he took
to spitting on the floor. Philip glanced at Lilia, but did not detect
her wincing. She talked bravely till the end of the disgusting meal,
and then got up saying: 'Well, Philip, I am sure you are ready
for bye-bye. We shall meet at twelve o'clock lunch tomorrow,
if we don't meet before. They give us *caffè-latte* in our rooms.'

It was a little too impudent. Philip replied, 'I should like to
see you now, please, in my room, as I have come all the way on
business.' He heard Miss Abbott gasp. Signor Carella, who was
lighting a rank cigar, had not understood.

It was as he expected. When he was alone with Lilia he
lost all nervousness. The remembrance of his long intellectual
supremacy strengthened him, and he began volubly –

'My dear Lilia, don't let's have a scene. Before I arrived I
thought I might have to question you. It is unnecessary. I know
everything. Miss Abbott has told me a certain amount, and the
rest I see for myself.'

'See for yourself?' she exclaimed, and he remembered afterwards that she had flushed crimson.

'That he is probably a ruffian and certainly a cad.'

'There are no cads in Italy,' she said quickly.

He was taken aback. It was one of his own remarks.

E. M. FORSTER
from *Where Angels Fear to Tread*

'He happy is, who farre from busie sounds'

He happy is, who farre from busie sounds,
   (As ancient mortals dwelt)
With his owne Oxen tills his Fathers grounds,
   And debts hath never felt.
No warre disturbes his rest with fierce alarmes,
   Nor angry Seas offend:
He shunnes the Law, and those ambitious charmes,
   Which great mens doores attend.
The lofty Poplers with delight he weds
   To Vines that grow apace,
And with his hooke unfruitfull branches shreds,
   More happy sprouts to place,
Or else beholds, how lowing heards astray,
   In narrow valleys creepe,
Or in cleane pots, doth pleasant hony lay,
   Or sheares his feeble Sheepe.
When Autumne from the ground his head upreares,
   With timely Apples chain'd,
How glad is he to plucke ingrafted Peares,
   And Grapes with purple stain'd?
Thus he Priapus, or Sylvanus payes,
   Who keepes his limits free,

His weary limbes, in holding grasse he layes,
    Or under some old tree,
Along the lofty bankes the waters slide,
    The Birds in woods lament,
The Springs with trickling streames the Ayre divide,
    Whence gentle sleepes are lent.
But when great Jove, in winters dayes restores
    Unpleasing showres and snowes,
With many Dogs he drives the angry Bores
    To snares which them oppose.
His slender nets dispos'd on little stakes,
    The greedy Thrush prevent:
The fearefull Hare, and forraine Crane he takes,
    With this reward content.
Who will not in these joyes forget the cares,
    Which oft in love we meete:
But when a modest wife the trouble shares
    Of house and children sweete,
Like Sabines, or the swift Apulians wives,
    Whose cheekes the Sun beames harme,
When from old wood she sacred fire contrives,
    Her weary mate to warme,
When she with hurdles, her glad flockes confines,
    And their full undders dries,
And from sweet vessels drawes the yearely wines,
    And meates unbought supplies;
No Lucrine Oysters can my palate please,
    Those fishes I neglect,
Which tempests thundring on the Easterne Seas
    Into our waves direct.
No Bird from Affrike sent, my taste allowes,
    Nor Fowle which Asia breeds:
The Olive (gather'd from the fatty boughes)
    With more delight me feeds.

Sowre Herbs, which love the Meades, or Mallowes good,
   To ease the body pain'd:
A Lambe which sheds to Terminus her blood,
   Or Kid from Wolves regain'd.
What joy is at these Feasts, when well-fed flocks
   Themselves for home prepare!
Or when the weake necke of the weary Oxe
   Drawes back th' inverted share!
When Slaves (the swarmes that wealthy houses charge)
   Neere smiling Lar, sit downe.
This life when Alphius hath describ'd at large,
   Inclining to the Clowne,
He at the Ides calles all that money in,
   Which he hath let for gaine:
But when the next month shall his course begin,
   He puts it out againe.

SIR JOHN BEAUMONT

'How happy in his low degree'

How happy in his low degree
How rich in humble Poverty, is he,
Who leads a quiet country life!
Discharg'd of business, void of strife,
And from the gripeing Scrivener free.
(Thus e're the Seeds of Vice were sown,
Liv'd Men in better Ages born,
Who Plow'd with Oxen of their own
Their small paternal field of Corn.)
Nor Trumpets summon him to War
   Nor drums disturb his morning Sleep,
Nor knows he Merchants gainful care,
   Nor fears the dangers of the deep.

The clamours of contentious Law,
   And Court and state he wisely shuns,
Nor brib'd with hopes nor dar'd with awe
   To servile Salutations runs:
But either to the clasping Vine
   Does the supporting Poplar Wed,
Or with his pruneing hook disjoyn
   Unbearing Branches from their Head,
   And grafts more happy in their stead:
Or climbing to a hilly Steep
   He views his Herds in Vales afar
Or Sheers his overburden'd Sheep,
   Or mead for cooling drink prepares,
   Of Virgin honey in the Jars.
Or in the now declining year
   When bounteous Autumn rears his head,
He joyes to pull the ripen'd Pear,
   And clustring Grapes with purple spread.
The fairest of his fruit he serves,
   Priapus thy rewards:
Sylvanus too his part deserves,
   Whose care the fences guards.
Sometimes beneath an ancient Oak,
   Or on the matted grass he lies;
No God of Sleep he need invoke,
   The stream that o're the pebbles flies
   With gentle slumber crowns his Eyes.
The Wind that Whistles through the sprays
   Maintains the consort of the Song;
And hidden Birds with native layes
   The golden sleep prolong.
But when the blast of Winter blows,
   And hoary frost inverts the year,
Into the naked Woods he goes

And seeks the tusky Boar to rear,
  With well mouth'd hounds and pointed Spear:
Or spreads his subtile Nets from sight
  With twinckling glasses to betray
The Larkes that in the Meshes light,
  Or makes the fearful Hare his prey.
Amidst his harmless easie joys
  No anxious care invades his health,
Nor Love his peace of mind destroys,
  Nor wicked avarice of Wealth.
But if a chast and pleasing Wife,
To ease the business of his Life,
Divides with him his houshold care,
Such as the Sabine Matrons were,
Such as the swift Apulians Bride,
  Sunburnt and Swarthy tho' she be,
Will fire for Winter Nights provide,
  And without noise will oversee,
  His Children and his Family,
And order all things till he come,
Sweaty and overlabour'd, home;
If she in pens his Flocks will fold,
  And then produce her Dairy store,
With Wine to drive away the cold,
  And unbought dainties of the poor;
Not Oysters of the Lucrine Lake
  My sober appetite wou'd wish,
  Nor Turbet, or the Foreign Fish
That rowling Tempests overtake,
  And hither waft the costly dish.
Not Heathpout, or the rarer Bird,
  Which Phasis, or Ionia yields,
More pleasing morsels wou'd afford
  Than the fat Olives of my fields;

Than Shards or Mallows for the pot,
　　That keep the loosen'd Body sound,
Or than the Lamb that falls by Lot,
　　To the just Guardian of my ground.
Amidst these feasts of happy Swains,
　　The jolly Shepheard smiles to see
His flock returning from the Plains;
　　The Farmer is as pleas'd as he
To view his Oxen, sweating smoak,
Bear on their Necks the loosen'd Yoke;
To look upon his menial Crew,
　　That sit around his cheerful hearth,
And bodies spent in toil renew
　　With wholesome Food and Country Mirth.
This Morecraft said within himself;
　　Resolv'd to leave the wicked Town,
　　And live retir'd upon his own;
He call'd his Mony in:
　　But the prevailing love of pelf,
　　Soon split him on the former shelf,
And put it out again.

JOHN DRYDEN

The Walrus and the
Carpenter

The sun was shining on the sea,
　　Shining with all his might:
He did his very best to make
　　The billows smooth and bright –
And this was odd, because it was
　　The middle of the night.

The moon was shining sulkily,
  Because she thought the sun
Had got no business to be there
  After the day was done –
'It's very rude of him,' she said,
  'To come and spoil the fun!'

The sea was wet as wet could be,
  The sands were dry as dry.
You could not see a cloud, because
  No cloud was in the sky:
No birds were flying overhead –
  There were no birds to fly.

The Walrus and the Carpenter
  Were walking close at hand:
They wept like anything to see
  Such quantities of sand:
'If this were only cleared away,
  They said, 'it *would* be grand!'

'If seven maids with seven mops
  Swept it for half a year,
Do you suppose,' the Walrus said,
  'That they could get it clear?'
'I doubt it,' said the Carpenter,
  And shed a bitter tear.

'O Oysters, come and walk with us!'
  The Walrus did beseech.
'A pleasant walk, a pleasant talk,
  Along the briny beach:
We cannot do with more than four,
  To give a hand to each.'

The eldest Oyster looked at him,
　　But never a word he said:
The eldest Oyster winked his eye,
　　And shook his heavy head –
Meaning to say he did not choose
　　To leave the oyster-bed.

But four young Oysters hurried up,
　　All eager for the treat:
Their coats were brushed, their faces washed,
　　Their shoes were clean and neat –
And this was odd, because, you know,
　　They hadn't any feet.

Four other oysters followed them,
　　And yet another four;
And thick and fast they came at last,
　　And more, and more, and more –
All hopping through the frothy waves,
　　And scrambling to the shore.

The Walrus and the Carpenter
　　Walked on a mile or so,
And then they rested on a rock
　　Conveniently low:
And all the little Oysters stood
　　And waited in a row.

'The time has come,' the Walrus said,
　　'To talk of many things:
Of shoes – and ships – and sealing-wax –
　　Of cabbages – and kings –
And why the sea is boiling hot –
　　And whether pigs have wings.'

'But wait a bit,' the Oysters cried,
　'Before we have our chat:
For some of us are out of breath,
　And all of us are fat!'
'No hurry!' said the Carpenter.
　They thanked him much for that.

'A loaf of bread,' the Walrus said,
　'Is what we chiefly need:
Pepper and vinegar besides
　Are very good indeed –
Now, if you're ready, Oysters dear,
　We can begin to feed.'

'But not on us!' the Oysters cried,
　Turning a little blue.
'After such kindness, that would be
　A dismal thing to do!'
'The night is fine,' the Walrus said.
　'Do you admire the view?

'It was so kind of you to come!
　And you are very nice!'
The Carpenter said nothing but
　'Cut us another slice.
I wish you were not quite so deaf –
　I've had to ask you twice!'

'It seems a shame,' the Walrus said,
　'To play them such a trick.
After we've brought them out so far,
　And made them trot so quick!'
The Carpenter said nothing but
　'The butter's spread too thick!'

'I weep for you,' the Walrus said:
'I deeply sympathize.'
With sobs and tears he sorted out
   Those of the largest size,
Holding his pocket-handkerchief
   Before his streaming eyes.

'O Oysters,' said the Carpenter,
   'You've had a pleasant run!
Shall we be trotting home again?'
   But answer came there none –
And this was scarcely odd, because
   They'd eaten every one.

LEWIS CARROLL
from *Alice's Adventures in Wonderland*

Country and Town

Shall I state the difference between my town grievances, and
my country comforts? At Brambleton-hall, I have elbow-room
within doors, and breathe a clear, elastic, salutary air – I enjoy
refreshing sleep, which is never disturbed by horrid noise, nor
interrupted, but in a-morning, by the sweet twitter of the martlet
at my window – I drink the virgin lymph, pure and chrystalline as
it gushes from the rock, or the sparkling beveridge, home-brewed
from malt of my own making; or I indulge with cyder, which
my own orchard affords; or with claret of the best growth,
imported for my own use, by a correspondent on whose integrity
I can depend; my bread is sweet and nourishing, made from
my own wheat, ground in my own mill, and baked in my own
oven; my table is, in a great measure, furnished from my own
ground; my five-year old mutton, fed on the fragrant herbage

of the mountains, that might vie with venison in juice and flavour; my delicious veal, fattened with nothing but the mother's milk, that fills the dish with gravy; my poultry from the barn-door, that never knew confinement, but when they were at roost; my rabbits panting from the warren; my game fresh from the moors; my trout and salmon struggling from the stream; oysters from their native banks; and herrings, with other sea fish, I can eat in four hours after they are taken – My sallads, roots, and pot-herbs, my own garden yields in plenty and perfection; the produce of the natural soil, prepared by moderate cultivation. The same soil affords all the different fruits which England may call her own, so that my dessert is every day fresh-gathered from the tree; my dairy flows with nectarious tides of milk and cream, from whence we derive abundance of excellent butter, curds, and cheese; and the refuse fattens my pigs, that are destined for hams and bacon – I go to bed betimes, and rise with the sun – I make shift to pass the hours without weariness or regret and am not destitute of amusements within doors, when the weather will not permit me to go abroad – I read, and chat, and play at billiards, cards or back-gammon – Without doors, I superintend my farm, and execute plans of improvements, the effects of which I enjoy with unspeakable delight – Nor do I take less pleasure in seeing my tenants thrive under my auspices, and the poor live comfortably by the employment which I provide – You know I have one or two sensible friends, to whom I can open all my heart; a blessing which, perhaps, I might have sought in vain among the crowded scenes of life: there are a few others of more humble parts, whom I esteem for their integrity; and their conversation I find inoffensive, though not very entertaining. Finally, I live in the midst of honest men, and trusty dependents, who, I flatter myself, have a disinterested attachment to my person – You, yourself, my dear Doctor, can vouch for the truth of these assertions.

Now, mark the contrast at London – I am pent up in frowzy lodgings, where there is not room enough to swing a cat; and I breathe the steams of endless putrefaction; and these would, undoubtedly, produce a pestilence, if they were not qualified by the gross acid of sea-coal, which is itself a pernicious nuisance to lungs of any delicacy of texture: but even this boasted corrector cannot prevent those languid, sallow looks, that distinguish the inhabitants of London from those ruddy swains that lead a country-life – I go to bed after midnight, jaded and restless from the dissipations of the day – I start every hour from my sleep, at the horrid noise of the watchmen bawling the hour through every street, and thundering at every door; a set of useless fellows, who serve no other purpose but that of disturbing the repose of the inhabitants; and by five o'clock I start out of bed, in consequence of the still more dreadful alarm made by the country carts, and noisy rustics bellowing green pease under my window. If I would drink water, I must quaff the maukish contents of an open aqueduct, exposed to all manner of defile-ment; or swallow that which comes from the river Thames, impregnated with all the filth of London and Westminster – Human excrement is the least offensive part of the concrete, which is composed of all the drugs, minerals, and poisons, used in mechanics and manufacture, enriched with the putrefying carcasses of beasts and men; and mixed with the scourings of all the wash-tubs, kennels, and common sewers, within the bills of mortality.

This is the agreeable potation, extolled by the Londoners, as the finest water in the universe – As to the intoxicating potion, sold for wine, it is a vile, unpalatable, and pernicious sophisti-cation, balderdashed with cyder, corn-spirit, and the juice of sloes. In an action at law, laid against a carman for having staved a cask of port, it appeared from the evidence of the cooper, that there were not above five gallons of real wine in the whole pipe, which held above a hundred, and even that had been brewed and adulterated by the merchant at Oporto. The bread I eat in London, is a deleterious paste, mixed up with chalk, alum, and bone-ashes; insipid to the taste, and destructive to the constitution. The good people are not ignorant of this adulteration; but they prefer it to wholesome bread, because it is whiter than the meal of corn: thus they sacrifice their taste and their health, and the lives of their tender infants, to a most absurd gratification of a mis-judging eye; and the miller, or the baker, is obliged to poison them and their families, in order to live by his profession. The same monstrous depravity appears in their veal, which is bleached by repeated bleedings, and other villainous arts, till there is not a drop of juice left in the body, and the poor animal is paralytic before it dies; so void of all taste, nourishment, and savour, that a man might dine as comfortably on a white fricassee of kid-skin gloves; or chip hats from Leghorn.

As they have discharged the natural colour from their bread, their butchers-meat, and poultry, their cutlets, ragouts, fricassees and sauces of all kinds; so they insist upon having the complexion of their pot-herbs mended, even at the hazard of their lives. Perhaps, you will hardly believe they can be so mad as to boil their greens with brass halfpence, in order to improve their colour; and yet nothing is more true – Indeed, without this improvement in the colour, they have no personal merit. They are produced in an artificial soil, and taste of nothing but the dunghills, from whence they spring. My cabbage, cauliflower, and 'sparagus in the country, are as much superior in flavour to those that are sold in Covent-garden, as my heath-mutton is to that of St James's-market; which in fact, is neither lamb nor mutton, but something betwixt the two, gorged in the rank fens of Lincoln and Essex, pale, coarse, and frowzy – As for the pork, it is an abominable carnivorous animal, fed with horse-flesh and distillers' grains; and the poultry is all rotten, in consequence of a fever, occasioned by the infamous practice of sewing up the gut, that they may be the sooner fattened in coops, in consequence of this cruel retention.

Of the fish, I need say nothing in this hot weather, but that it comes sixty, seventy, fourscore, and a hundred miles by land-carriage; a circumstance sufficient without any comment, to turn a Dutchman's stomach, even if his nose was not saluted in every alley with the sweet flavour of *fresh* mackarel, selling by retail – This is not the season for oysters; nevertheless, it may not be amiss to mention, that the right Colchester are kept in slime-pits, occasionally overflowed by the sea; and that the green colour, so much admired by the voluptuaries of this metropolis, is occasioned by the vitriolic scum, which rises on the surface of the stagnant and stinking water – Our rabbits are bred and fed in the poulterer's cellar, where they have neither air nor exercise, consequently they must be firm in flesh, and delicious in flavour; and there is no game to be had for love or money.

It must be owned, the Covent-garden affords some good fruit; which, however, is always engrossed by a few individuals of overgrown fortune, at an exorbitant price; so that little else than the refuse of the market falls to the share of the community; and that is distributed by such filthy hands, as I cannot look at without loathing. It was but yesterday that I saw a dirty barrow-bunter in the street, cleaning her dusty fruit with her own spittle; and, who knows but some fine lady of St James's parish might admit into her delicate mouth those very cherries, which had been rolled and moistened between the filthy, and, perhaps, ulcerated chops of a St Giles's huckster – I need not dwell upon the pallid, contaminated mash, which they call strawberries; soiled and tossed by greasy paws through twenty baskets crusted with dirt; and then presented with the worst milk, thickened with the worst flour, into a bad likeness of cream: but the milk itself should not pass unanalysed, the produce of faded cabbage-leaves and sour draff, lowered with hot water, frothed with bruised snails, carried through the streets in open pails, exposed to foul rinsings, discharged from doors and windows, spittle, snot, and tobacco-quids from foot passengers, overflowings from mud carts, spatterings from coach wheels, dirt and trash chucked into it by roguish boys for the joke's sake, the spewings of infants, who have slabbered in the tin-measure, which is thrown back in that condition among the milk, for the benefit of the next customer; and, finally, the vermin that drops from the rags of the nasty drab that vends this precious mixture, under the respectable denomination of milk-maid.

I shall conclude this catalogue of London dainties, with that table-beer, guiltless of hops and malt, vapid and nauseous; much fitter to facilitate the operation of a vomit, than to quench thirst and promote digestion; the tallowy rancid mass, called butter, manufactured with candle grease and kitchen stuff; and their fresh eggs, imported from France and Scotland. – Now, all these enormities might be remedied with a very little attention to the article of police, or civil regulation; but the wise patriots of London have taken it into their heads, that all regulation is inconsistent with liberty; and that every man ought to live in his own way, without restraint – Nay, as there is not sense enough left among them, to be discomposed by the nuisance I have mentioned, they may, for aught I care, wallow in the mire of their own pollution.

TOBIAS SMOLLETT

from *Humphry Clinker*

A Songe bewailinge the tyme of Christmas, So much decayed in Englande

Christmas is my name, Farr have I gone, have I gone, have
  I gone,
have I gone without regarde,
  Whereas great men, by flockes they be flowen, they be
    flowen
they be flowen, they be flowen to London warde,
  Where they in pompe, and pleasure do waste,
that which Christmas had wont to feast
              Wellay daie.
Houses where musicke was wonted to ringe,
  Nothinge but Batts, and Ouls now do singe
Wellay daie, wallay daie, wallay daie, where should I stay.

  Christmas bread and Beefe, is turnd into stons, into stons,
    into stons,
Into Stones and Silken ragges.
  And ladie monie it doth slepe, It doth slepe, It doth sleepe,
It doth sleepe in Mysers bagges.
  Where manie gallantes once abounde,
Nought but A dogg and A Sheperd is founde,
              Wellay day.
Places where Christmas revells did keepe,
  Are now becom habitations for Sheepe.
Wallay day, wallay day, wellay day, where should I stay.

  Pan the Shepherdes God, doth deface, doth deface, doth
    deface,
doth deface, Ladie Ceres crowne,
  And Tilliges doth decay, doth decay, doth decay,
doth decay in everie towne.

Landlordes their rentes so highly Inhaunce,
That Peares the plowman, barefoot doth daunce,
   Wellay day.
Farmers that Christmas woulde Intertaine,
 hath scarselie withall them selves to maintaine,
Wellay day, wellay day, wellay day, where should I stay.

Go to the Protestant, hele protest, hele protest, hele
  protest,
he will protest and bouldlie boaste,
 And to the Puritine, he is so hote, he is so hote, he is so
  hote,
he is so hote he will burne the Roast,
 The Catholike good deeds will not scorne,
nor will not see pore Christmas forlorne,
   Wellay Day.
Since Holines no good deedes will do,
 Protestantes had best turn Papistes too,
Wellay day, Wellay day, wellay day, where should I stay.

Pride and Luxurie, doth devoure, doth devoure, doth
  devoure,
doth devour house kepinge quite,
 And Beggarie, doth beget, doth begett, doth begett,
doth begett in manie A knight.
 Madam for sooth in Cooch she must reele
Although she weare her hoose out at heele,
   Wellay day.
And on her backe were that for her weede,
 that woulde both me, and manie other feede,
Wellay day, Wallay day, wellay day, where should I stay.

 Breefelye for to ende, here I fynde, here I fynde,
here I fynde such great vacation

That some great houses, do seeme to have, Seme to have,
    seeme to have,
for to have some great Purgation,
  With Purginge Pills, such effectes they have Shewed,
that out of dores, theyr owners they have spewed.
               Wellay day.
And when Christmas goes by and calles,
  Nothinge but solitude, and naked walls,
Wellay day, Wellay day, wellay day, where should I staie.

Philemels Cottages are turnd into gould, into gould,
Into gould for harboringe Jove.
  And great mens houses up for to hould, up for to houlde,
up for to hould, make great men mone,
  But in the Cittie they saie they do live,
Where gould by handfulls away they do give
               Wellay day.
And therefore thither I purpose to passe,
  hopinge at london to fynde the goulden Asse,
Ile away, Ile away, Ile away, Ile no longer staie.

ANONYMOUS

Queen Eleanor and her Dwarf

Dwerga:

What, am I not thy grandchild? thou that bought'st me
Of my Norse dam, when scarce the size of a crab,
And fed'st me to my present stature with
Dainties of all kinds – cock's eggs, and young frogs
So freshly caught they whistled as they singed,
Like moist wood, on the spit, still bubbling out

Dew from their liquid ribs, to baste themselves,
As they turn'd slowly – then rich snails that slip
My throttle down ere I well savour them;
Most luscious mummy; bat's milk cheese; at times
The sweetbreads of fall'n mooncalves, or the jellies
Scumm'd after shipwreck floating to the shore:
Have I not eat live mandrakes, screaming torn
From their warm churchyard-bed, out of thy hand?
With other roots and fruits cull'd ere their season –
The yew's green berries, nightshade's livid bugles,
That poison human chits but nourish me –
False mushrooms, toadstools, oakwarts, hemlock chopt?

Eleanor:

Ay, thou 'rt an epicure in such luxuries.

Dwerga:

My fangs still water! – Grandam, thou art good!
Dost thou not give me daily for my draught
Pure sloe-juice, bitter-sweet! or wormwood wine,
Syrup of galls, old coffin-snags boil'd down
Thrice in fat charnel-juice, so strong and hilarious,
I dance to a tub's sound like the charmer's snake,
We at Aleppo saw? What made me, pray you,
All that I am, but this fine food? Thou art,
Then, my creatress; and I am thy creature.

GEORGE DARLEY

Flesh and Fat

I have found repeatedly, of late years, that I cannot fish without
falling a little in self-respect. I have tried it again and again. I
have skill at it, and, like many of my fellows, a certain instinct
for it, which revives from time to time, but always when I have
done I feel that it would have been better if I had not fished. I
think that I do not mistake. It is a faint intimation, yet so are
the first streaks of morning. There is unquestionably this instinct
in me which belongs to the lower orders of creation; yet with
every year I am less a fisherman, though without more humanity
or even wisdom; at present I am no fisherman at all. But I see
that if I were to live in a wilderness I should again be tempted
to become a fisher and hunter in earnest. Beside, there is
something essentially unclean about this diet and all flesh, and
I began to see where housework commences, and whence the
endeavor, which costs so much, to wear a tidy and respectable
appearance each day, to keep the house sweet and free from all
ill odors and sights. Having been my own butcher and scullion
and cook, as well as the gentleman for whom the dishes were
served up, I can speak from an unusually complete experience.
The practical objection to animal food in my case was its
uncleanness; and, besides, when I had caught and cleaned and
cooked and eaten my fish, they seemed not to have fed me
essentially. It was insignificant and unnecessary, and cost more
than it came to. A little bread or a few potatoes would have
done as well, with less trouble and filth. Like many of my
contemporaries, I had rarely for many years used animal food,
or tea, or coffee, &c.; not so much because of any ill effects
which I had traced to them, as because they were not agreeable
to my imagination. The repugnance to animal food is not the
effect of experience, but is an instinct. It appeared more beautiful
to live low and fare hard in many respects; and though I never

did so, I went far enough to please my imagination. I believe that every man who has ever been earnest to preserve his higher or poetic faculties in the best condition has been particularly inclined to abstain from animal food, and from much food of any kind. It is a significant fact, stated by entomologists, I find it in Kirby and Spence, that 'some insects in their perfect state, though furnished with organs of feeding, make no use of them'; and they lay it down as 'a general rule, that almost all insects in this state eat much less than in that of larvæ. The voracious caterpillar when transformed into a butterfly' ... 'and the gluttonous maggot when become a fly', content themselves with a drop or two of honey or some other sweet liquid. The abdomen under the wings of the butterfly still represents the larva. This is the tid-bit which tempts his insectivorous fate. The gross feeder is a man in the larva state; and there are whole nations in that condition, nations without fancy or imagination, whose vast abdomens betray them.

It is hard to provide and cook so simple and clean a diet as will not offend the imagination; but this, I think, is to be fed when we feed the body; they should both sit down at the same table. Yet perhaps this may be done. The fruits eaten temperately need not make us ashamed of our appetites, nor interrupt the worthiest pursuits. But put an extra condiment into your dish, and it will poison you. It is not worth the while to live by rich cookery. Most men would feel shame if caught preparing with their own hands precisely such a dinner, whether of animal or vegetable food, as is every day prepared for them by others. Yet till this is otherwise we are not civilized, and, if gentlemen and ladies, are not true men and women. This certainly suggests what change is to be made. It may be vain to ask why the imagination will not be reconciled to flesh and fat. I am satisfied that it is not. Is it not a reproach that man is a carnivorous animal? True, he can and does live, in a great measure, by preying on other animals; but this is a miserable way – as any one who will go to snaring rabbits, or slaughtering lambs, may learn – and he will be regarded as a benefactor of his race who shall teach man to confine himself to a more innocent and wholesome diet. Whatever my own practice may be, I have no doubt that it is a part of the destiny of the human race, in its gradual improvement, to leave off eating animals, as surely as the savage tribes have left off eating each other when they came in contact with the more civilized.

HENRY DAVID THOREAU
from *Walden*

'The húman skull is of deceít'

The húman skull is of deceit
As fúll as any egg of meat;
Fúll of deceít's the human skull
As ány egg of meat is full.
Some eggs are addled, some are sweet,
But évery egg's chokefúl of meat;
Cléver some skúlls, some skulls are dull,
Bút of deceít each skull's chokeful.
Lét your egg áddled be or sweet,
To háve your éggshell clean and neat
The first step is: scoop out the meat;
And cléver let it be or dull,
If you would háve an honest skull,
Oút you must scrape to the last grain
The vile, false, lýing, pérjured brain.

JAMES HENRY

Flies, Spiders and a Sparrow

Dr Seward's Diary

5 June. – The case of Renfield grows more interesting the more I get to understand the man. He has certain qualities very largely developed: selfishness, secrecy, and purpose. I wish I could get at what is the object of the latter. He seems to have some settled scheme of his own, but what it is I do not yet know. His redeeming quality is a love of animals, though, indeed, he has such curious turns in it that I sometimes imagine he is only abnormally cruel. His pets are of odd sorts. Just now his hobby is catching flies. He has at present such a quantity that I have had myself to expostulate. To my astonishment, he did not break out into a fury, as I expected, but took the matter in simple seriousness. He thought for a moment, and then said: 'May I have three days? I shall clear them away.' Of course, I said that would do. I must watch him.

18 June. – He has turned his mind now to spiders, and has got several very big fellows in a box. He keeps feeding them with his flies, and the number of the latter is becoming sensibly diminished, although he has used half his food in attracting more flies from outside to his room.

1 July. – His spiders are now becoming as great a nuisance as his flies, and to-day I told him that he must get rid of them. He looked very sad at this, so I said that he must clear out some of them, at all events. He cheerfully acquiesced in this, and I gave him the same time as before for reduction. He disgusted me much while with him, for when a horrid blowfly, bloated with some carrion food, buzzed into the room, he caught it, held it exultingly for a few moments between his finger and thumb, and, before I knew what he was going to do, put it in his mouth and ate it. I scolded him for it, but he argued quietly that it was very good and very wholesome; that it was life, strong life, and gave life to him. This gave me an idea, or the rudiment of one. I must watch how he gets rid of his spiders. He has evidently some deep problem in his mind, for he keeps a little note-book in which he is always jotting down something. Whole pages are filled with masses of figures, generally single numbers added up in batches, and then the totals added in batches again, as though he was 'focusing' some account, as the auditors put it.

8 July. – There is a method in his madness, and the rudimentary idea in my mind is growing. It will be a whole idea soon, and then, oh, unconscious celebration! you will have to give the wall to your conscious brother. I kept away from my friend for a few days, so that I might notice if there were any change. Things remained as they were except that he has parted with some of his pets and got a new one. He has managed to get a sparrow, and has already partially tamed it. His means of taming is simple, for already the spiders have diminished. Those that do remain, however, are well fed, for he still brings in the flies by tempting them with his food.

BRAM STOKER

Turkish Leisure

I am at this present writing in a House situate on the banks of the Hebrus, which runs under my Chamber Window. My Garden is full of Tall Cypress Trees, upon the branches of which several Couple of true Turtles are saying soft things to one another from Morning till night. How naturally do boughs and vows come into my head at this minute! And must not you confess to my praise that tis more than an ordinary Discretion that can resist the wicked Suggestions of Poetry in a place where Truth for once furnishes all the Ideas of Pastorall? The Summer is allready far advanc'd in this part of the World, and for some miles round Adrianople the whole ground is laid out in Gardens, and the Banks of the River set with Rows of Fruit trees, under which all the most considerable Turks divert them selves every Evening; not with walking, that is not one of their Pleasures, but a set party of 'em chuse out a green spot where the Shade is very thick, and there they spread a carpet on which they sit drinking their Coffee and generally attended by some slave with a fine voice or that plays on some instrument. Every 20 paces you may see one of these little companys listening to the dashing of the river, and this taste is so universal that the very Gardiners are not without it. I have often seen them and their children sitting on the banks and playing on a rural Instrument perfectly answering the description of the Ancient Fistula, being compos'd of unequal reeds, with a simple but agreable softness in the Sound. Mr Adison might here make the Experiment he speaks of in his travells, there not being one instrument of music among the Greek or Roman statues that is not to be found in the hands of the people of this country. The young Lads gennerally divert themselves with makeing Girlands for their favourite Lambs, which I have often seen painted and adorn'd with flowers, lying at their feet while they sung or play'd. It is not that they ever read Romances, but these are the Ancient Amusements here, and as natural to them as Cudgel playing and football to our British Swains, the softness and warmth of the Climate forbiding all rough Exercises, which were never so much as heard of amongst 'em, and naturally inspiring a Lazyness and aversion to Labour, which the great Plenty indulges. These Gardiners are the only happy race of Country people in Turkey. They furnish all the City with Fruit and herbs, and seem to live very easily. They are most of 'em Greeks and have little Houses in the midst of their Gardens where their Wives and daughters take a Liberty not permitted in the Town: I mean, to go unavail'd. These Wenches are very neat and handsome, and pass their time at their Looms under the shade of their Trees. I no longer look upon Theocritus as a Romantic Writer; he has only given a plain image of the Way of Life amongst the Peasants of his Country, which before oppresion had reduc'd them to want, were I suppose all employ'd as the better sort of 'em are now. I don't doubt he had been born a Briton his Idylliums had been fill'd with Descriptions of Thrashing and churning, both which are unknown here, the Corn being all trod out by Oxen, and Butter (I speak it with sorrow) unheard of.

LADY MARY WORTLEY MONTAGU

At the Maypole

One wintry evening, early in the year of our Lord one thousand seven hundred and eighty, a keen north wind arose as it grew dark, and night came on with black and dismal looks. A bitter storm of sleet, sharp, dense, and icy-cold, swept the wet streets, and rattled on the trembling windows. Signboards, shaken past endurance in their creaking frames, fell crashing on the pavement; old tottering chimneys reeled and staggered in the blast; and many a steeple rocked again that night, as though the earth were troubled.

It was not a time for those who could by any means get light and warmth, to brave the fury of the weather. In coffee-houses of the better sort, guests crowded round the fire, forgot to be political, and told each other with a secret gladness that the blast grew fiercer every minute. Each humble tavern by the water-side, had its group of uncouth figures round the hearth, who talked of vessels foundering at sea, and all hands lost; related many a dismal tale of shipwreck and drowned men, and hoped that some they knew were safe, and shook their heads in doubt. In private dwellings, children clustered near the blaze; listening with timid pleasure to tales of ghosts and goblins, and tall figures clad in white standing by bedsides, and people who had gone to sleep in old churches and being overlooked had found themselves alone there at the dead hour of the night: until they shuddered at the thought of the dark rooms upstairs, yet loved to hear the wind moan too, and hoped it would continue bravely. From time to time these happy indoor people stopped to listen, or one held up his finger and cried 'Hark!' and then, above the rumbling in the chimney, and the fast pattering on the glass, was heard a wailing, rushing sound, which shook the walls as though a giant's hand were on them; then a hoarse roar as if the sea had risen; then such a whirl and tumult that the air seemed mad; and then, with a lengthened howl, the waves of wind swept on, and left a moment's interval of rest.

Cheerily, though there were none abroad to see it, shone the Maypole light that evening. Blessings on the red – deep, ruby, glowing red – old curtain of the window; blending into one rich stream of brightness, fire and candle, meat, drink, and company, and gleaming like a jovial eye upon the bleak waste out of doors! Within, what carpet like its crunching sand, what music merry as its crackling logs, what perfume like its kitchen's dainty breath, what weather genial as its hearty warmth! Blessings on the old house, how sturdily it stood! How did the vexed wind chafe and roar about its stalwart roof; how did it pant and strive with its wide chimneys, which still poured forth from their hospitable throats, great clouds of smoke, and puffed defiance in its face; how, above all, did it drive and rattle at the casement, emulous to extinguish that cheerful glow, which would not be put down and seemed the brighter for the conflict!

The profusion too, the rich and lavish bounty, of that goodly tavern! It was not enough that one fire roared and sparkled on its spacious hearth; in the tiles which paved and compassed it, five hundred flickering fires burnt brightly also. It was not enough that one red curtain shut the wild night out, and shed its cheerful influence on the room. In every saucepan lid, and candlestick, and vessel of copper, brass, or tin that hung upon the walls, were countless ruddy hangings, flashing and gleaming with every motion of the blaze, and offering, let the eye wander where it might, interminable vistas of the same rich colour. The old oak wainscoting, the beams, the chairs, the seats, reflected it in a deep, dull glimmer. There were fires and red curtains in the very eyes of the drinkers, in their buttons, in their liquor, in the pipes they smoked.

CHARLES DICKENS
from *Barnaby Rudge*

'In leathern jack to drink much less I hate'

In leathern jack* to drink much less I hate,
Than in Sir William's antique set of plate.
He tells the gasconading pedigree,
Till the wine turns insipid too as he.
This tumbler, in the world the oldest toy,
Says he, was brought by Brute himself from Troy.
That handled cup, and which is larger far,
A present to my father from the Czar:
See how 'tis bruis'd, and the work broken off;
'Twas when he flung it at prince Menzicoff.
The other with the cover, which is less,
Was once the property of good queen Bess:
In it she pledg'd duke d'Alençon, then gave it
To Drake, my wife's great uncle: so we have it

* jug

The bowl, the tankard, flagon, and the beaker,
Were my great-grandfather's, when he was speaker.
What pity 'tis, that plate so old and fine,
Should correspond no better with the wine.

WILLIAM HAY

The Custard

For second course, last night, a Custard came
To th' board, so hot, as none co'd touch the same:
Furze, three or foure times with his cheeks did blow
Upon the Custard, and thus cooled so:
It seem'd by this time to admit the touch;
But none co'd eate it, 'cause it stunk so much.

ROBERT HERRICK

To One that had Meate Ill Drest

King Mithridate to poysons so inur'd him,
As deadly poysons, damage none procur'd him.
So you to stale vnsauorie foode and durtie,
Are so inur'd, as famine ne'er can hurt yee.

SIR JOHN HARINGTON

To Ligurinus

The single cause why you invite,
Is that your works you may recite.
I hardly had my slippers dropt,
Nor dremt the entertainment stopt;
When, mid the lettuces and sallad,
Is usher'd in a bloody ballad.
Then lo! another bunch of lays,
While yet the primal service stays.
Another, ere the second course!
A third, and fourth, and fifth you force.
The boar, beroasted now to rags,
Appears in vain: the stomach flags.
The labors, that destroy each dish,
Were usefull coats for frying fish.
Affirm, my BARD, this dire decree:
Else you shall sup alone for me.

JAMES ELPHINSTON

To Classicus

When thou art ask'd to Sup abroad,
    Thou swear'st thou hast but newly din'd;
That eating late does overload
    The Stomach, and oppress the Mind;
But if *Appicius* makes a Treat,
    The slend'rest Summons thou obey'st,
No Child is greedier of the Teat,
    Than thou art of the bounteous Feast.

Then wilt thou drink till every Star
 Be swallow'd by the rising Sun:
Such Charms hath Wine we pay not for,
 And Mirth, at others Charge begun.
Who shuns his Club, yet flies to ev'ry Treat
 Does not a Supper, but a Reck'ning hate.

SIR CHARLES SEDLEY

First Breakfast at Sea

At eight o'clock the bell was struck, and we went to breakfast.
And now some of the worst of my troubles began. For not
having had any friend to tell me what I would want at sea, I
had not provided myself, as I should have done, with a good
many things that a sailor needs; and for my own part, it had
never entered my mind, that sailors had no table to sit down
to, no cloth, or napkins, or tumblers, and had to provide every
thing themselves. But so it was.

The first thing they did was this. Every sailor went to the
cook-house with his tin pot, and got it filled with coffee; but of
course, having no pot, there was no coffee for me. And after
that, a sort of little tub called a 'kid', was passed down into the
forecastle, filled with something they called 'burgoo'. This was
like mush, made of Indian corn meal and water. With the 'kid',
a little tin cannikin was passed down with molasses. Then the
Jackson that I spoke of before, put the kid between his knees,
and began to pour in the molasses, just like an old landlord
mixing punch for a party. He scooped out a little hole in the
middle of the mush, to hold the molasses; so it looked for all
the world like a little black pool in the Dismal Swamp of Virginia.

Then they all formed a circle round the kid; and one after
the other, with great regularity, dipped their spoons into the

mush, and after stirring them round a little in the molasses-pool, they swallowed down their mouthfuls, and smacked their lips over it, as if it tasted very good; which I have no doubt it did; but not having any spoon, I wasn't sure.

I sat some time watching these proceedings, and wondering how polite they were to each other; for, though there were a great many spoons to only one dish, they never got entangled. At last, seeing that the mush was getting thinner and thinner, and that it was getting low water, or rather low molasses in the little pool, I ran on deck, and after searching about, returned with a bit of stick; and thinking I had as good a right as any one else to the mush and molasses, I worked my way into the circle, intending to make one of the party. So I shoved in my stick, and after twirling it about, was just managing to carry a little *burgoo* toward my mouth, which had been for some time standing ready open to receive it, when one of the sailors perceiving what I was about, knocked the stick out of my hands, and asked me where I learned my manners; Was that the way gentlemen eat in my country? Did they eat their victuals with splinters of wood, and couldn't that wealthy gentleman my father afford to buy his gentlemanly son a spoon?

All the rest joined in, and pronounced me an ill-bred, coarse, and unmannerly youngster, who, if permitted to go on with such behavior as that, would corrupt the whole crew, and make them no better than swine.

As I felt conscious that a stick was indeed a thing very unsuitable to eat with, I did not say much to this, though it vexed me enough; but remembering that I had seen one of the steerage passengers with a pan and spoon in his hand eating his breakfast on the fore hatch, I now ran on deck again, and to my great joy succeeded in borrowing his spoon, for he had got through his meal, and down I came again, though at the eleventh hour, and offered myself once more as a candidate.

But alas! there was little more of the Dismal Swamp left, and when I reached over to the opposite end of the kid, I received a rap on the knuckles from a spoon, and was told that I must help myself from my own side, for that was the rule. But *my* side was scraped clean, so I got no *burgoo* that morning.

But I made it up by eating some salt beef and biscuit, which I found to be the invariable accompaniment of every meal; the sailors sitting cross-legged on their chests in a circle, and breaking the hard biscuit, very sociably, over each other's heads, which was very convenient indeed, but gave me the headache, at least for the first four or five days till I got used to it; and then I did not care much about it, only it kept my hair full of crumbs; and I had forgot to bring a fine comb and brush, so I used to shake my hair out to windward over the bulwarks every evening.

HERMAN MELVILLE
from *Redburn*

Smallweed, Jobling and Guppy at Dinner

Accordingly they betake themselves to a neighbouring dining-house, of the class known among its frequenters by the denomination Slap-Bang, where the waitress, a bouncing young female of forty, is supposed to have made some impression on the susceptible Smallweed; of whom it may be remarked that he is a weird changeling, to whom years are nothing. He stands precociously possessed of centuries of owlish wisdom. If he ever lay in a cradle, it seems as if he must have lain there in a tail-coat. He has an old, old eye, has Smallweed; and he drinks, and smokes, in a monkeyish way; and his neck is stiff in his collar; and he is never to be taken in; and he knows all about it, whatever it is. In short, in his bringing up, he has been so nursed by Law and Equity that he has become a kind of fossil Imp, to account for whose terrestrial existence it is reported at the public offices that his father was John Doe, and his mother the only female member of the Roe family, also that his first long-clothes were made from a blue bag.

Into the Dining House, unaffected by the seductive show in the window, of artificially whitened cauliflowers and poultry, verdant baskets of peas, coolly blooming cucumbers, and joints ready for the spit, Mr Smallweed leads the way. They know him there, and defer to him. He has his favourite box, he bespeaks all the papers, he is down upon bald patriarchs, who keep them more than ten minutes afterwards. It is of no use trying him with anything less than a full-sized 'bread', or proposing to him any joint in cut, unless it is in the very best cut. In the matter of gravy he is adamant.

Conscious of his elfin power, and submitting to his dread experience, Mr Guppy consults him in the choice of that day's banquet; turning an appealing look towards him as the waitress repeats the catalogue of viands, and saying 'What do *you* take, Chick?' Chick, out of the profundity of his artfulness, preferring 'veal and ham and French beans – And don't you forget the stuffing, Polly' (with an unearthly cock of his venerable eye); Mr Guppy and Mr Jobling give the like order. Three pint pots of half-and-half are superadded. Quickly the waitress returns, bearing what is apparently a model of the tower of Babel, but what is really a pile of plates and flat tin dish-covers. Mr Smallweed, approving of what is set before him, conveys intelligent benignity into his ancient eye, and winks upon her. Then, amid a constant coming in, and going out, and running about, and a clatter of crockery, and a rumbling up and down of the machine which brings the nice cuts from the kitchen, and a shrill crying for more nice cuts down the speaking-pipe, and a shrill reckoning of the cost of nice cuts that have been disposed of, and a general flush and steam of hot joints, cut and uncut, and a considerably heated atmosphere in which the soiled knives and table-cloths seem to break out spontaneously into eruptions of grease and blotches of beer, the legal triumvirate appease their appetites.

Mr Jobling is buttoned up closer than mere adornment might require. His hat presents at the rims a peculiar appearance of a glistening nature, as if it had been a favourite snail-promenade. The same phenomenon is visible on some parts of his coat, and particularly at the seams. He has the faded appearance of a gentleman in embarrassed circumstances; even his light whiskers droop with something of a shabby air.

His appetite is so vigorous, that it suggests spare living for some little time back. He makes such a speedy end of his plate of veal and ham, bringing it to a close while his companions are yet midway in theirs, that Mr Guppy proposes another. 'Thank you, Guppy,' says Mr Jobling, 'I really don't know but what I *will* take another.'

Another being brought, he falls to with great good will.

Mr Guppy takes silent notice of him at intervals, until he is half way through this second plate and stops to take an enjoying pull at his pint pot of half-and-half (also renewed), and stretches out his legs and rubs his hands. Beholding him in which glow of contentment, Mr Guppy says:

'You are a man again, Tony!'

'Well, not quite, yet,' says Mr Jobling. 'Say, just born.'

'Will you take any other vegetables? Grass? Peas? Summer cabbage?'

'Thank you, Guppy,' says Mr Jobling. 'I really don't know but what I *will* take summer cabbage.'

Order given; with the sarcastic addition (from Mr Smallweed) of 'Without slugs, Polly!' And cabbage produced.

'I am growing up, Guppy,' says Mr Jobling, plying his knife and fork with a relishing steadiness.

'Glad to hear it.'

'In fact, I have just turned into my teens,' says Mr Jobling.

He says no more until he has performed his task, which he

achieves as Messrs Guppy and Smallweed finish theirs; thus getting over the ground in excellent style, and beating those two gentlemen easily by a veal and ham and a cabbage.

'Now, Small,' says Mr Guppy, 'what would you recommend about pastry?'

'Marrow puddings,' says Mr Smallweed instantly.

'Aye, aye!' cries Mr Jobling, with an arch look. 'You're there, are you? Thank you, Guppy, I don't know but what I *will* take a marrow pudding.'

Three marrow puddings being produced, Mr Jobling adds, in a pleasant humour, that he is coming of age fast. To these succeed, by command of Mr Smallweed, 'three Cheshires'; and to those, 'three small rums'. This apex of the entertainment happily reached, Mr Jobling puts up his legs on the carpeted seat (having his own side of the box to himself), leans against the wall, and says, 'I am grown up, now, Guppy. I have arrived at maturity.'

CHARLES DICKENS
from *Bleak House*

Goblin Market

Morning and evening
Maids heard the goblins cry:
'Come buy our orchard fruits,
Come buy, come buy:
Apples and quinces,
Lemons and oranges,
Plump unpecked cherries,
Melons and raspberries,
Bloom-down-cheeked peaches,
Swart-headed mulberries,
Wild free-born cranberries,

Crab-apples, dewberries,
Pine-apples, blackberries,
Apricots, strawberries –
All ripe together
In summer weather –
Morns that pass by,
Fair eves that fly;
Come buy, come buy:
Our grapes fresh from the vine,
Pomegranates full and fine,
Dates and sharp bullaces,
Rare pears and greengages,
Damsons and bilberries,
Taste them and try:
Currants and gooseberries,
Bright-fire-like barberries,
Figs to fill your mouth,
Citrons from the South,
Sweet to tongue and sound to eye;
Come buy, come buy.'

Evening by evening
Among the brookside rushes,
Laura bowed her head to hear,
Lizzie veiled her blushes:
Crouching close together
In the cooling weather,
With clasping arms and cautioning lips,
With tingling cheeks and finger tips.
'Lie close,' Laura said,
Pricking up her golden head:
'We must not look at goblin men,
We must not buy their fruits:

Who knows upon what soil they fed
Their hungry thirsty roots?'
'Come buy,' call the goblins
Hobbling down the glen.
'Oh,' cried Lizzie, 'Laura, Laura,
You should not peep at goblin men.'
Lizzie covered up her eyes,
Covered close lest they should look;
Laura reared her glossy head,
And whispered like the restless brook:
'Look, Lizzie, look, Lizzie,
Down the glen tramp little men.
One hauls a basket,
One bears a plate,
One lugs a golden dish
Of many pounds' weight.
How fair the vine must grow
Whose grapes are so luscious;
How warm the wind must blow
Through those fruit bushes.'
'No,' said Lizzie: 'No, no, no;
Their offers should not charm us,
Their evil gifts would harm us.'
She thrust a dimpled finger
In each ear, shut eyes and ran:
Curious Laura chose to linger
Wondering at each merchant man.

One had a cat's face,
One whisked a tail,
One tramped at a rat's pace,
One crawled like a snail,
One like a wombat prowled obtuse and furry,
One like a ratel tumbled hurry skurry.

She heard a voice like voice of doves
Cooing all together:
They sounded kind and full of loves
In the pleasant weather.

Laura stretched her gleaming neck
Like a rush-imbedded swan,
Like a lily from the beck,
Like a moonlit poplar branch,
Like a vessel at the launch
When its last restraint is gone.

Backwards up the mossy glen
Turned and trooped the goblin men,
With their shrill repeated cry,
'Come buy, come buy.'
When they reached where Laura was
They stood stock still upon the moss,
Leering at each other,
Brother with queer brother;
Signalling each other,
Brother with sly brother.
One set his basket down,
One reared his plate;
One began to weave a crown
Of tendrils, leaves and rough nuts brown
(Men sell not such in any town);
One heaved the golden weight
Of dish and fruit to offer her:
'Come buy, come buy,' was still their cry.
Laura stared but did not stir,
Longed but had no money:
The whisk-tailed merchant bade her taste
In tones as smooth as honey,

The cat-faced purr'd,
The rat-paced spoke a word
Of welcome, and the snail-paced even was heard;
One parrot-voiced and jolly
Cried 'Pretty Goblin' still for 'Pretty Polly' –
One whistled like a bird.

But sweet-tooth Laura spoke in haste:
'Good Folk, I have no coin;
To take were to purloin:
I have no copper in my purse,
I have no silver either,
And all my gold is on the furze
That shakes in windy weather
Above the rusty heather.'
'You have much gold upon your head,'
They answered all together:
'Buy from us with a golden curl.'
She clipped a precious golden lock,
She dropped a tear more rare than pearl,
Then sucked their fruit globes fair or red:
Sweeter than honey from the rock,
Stronger than man-rejoicing wine,
Clearer than water flowed that juice;
She never tasted such before,
How should it cloy with length of use?
She sucked and sucked and sucked the more
Fruits which that unknown orchard bore;
She sucked until her lips were sore;
Then flung the emptied rinds away
But gathered up one kernel-stone,
And knew not was it night or day
As she turned home alone.

Lizzie met her at the gate
Full of wise upbraidings:
'Dear, you should not stay so late,
Twilight is not good for maidens;
Should not loiter in the glen
In the haunts of goblin men.
Do you not remember Jeanie,
How she met them in the moonlight,
Took their gifts both choice and many,
Ate their fruits and wore their flowers
Plucked from bowers
Where summer ripens at all hours?
But ever in the noonlight
She pined and pined away;
Sought them by night and day,
Found them no more but dwindled and grew grey;
Then fell with the first snow,
While to this day no grass will grow
Where she lies low:
I planted daisies there a year ago
That never blow.
You should not loiter so.'
'Nay, hush,' said Laura:
'Nay, hush, my sister:
I ate and ate my fill,
Yet my mouth waters still;
To-morrow night I will
Buy more:' and kissed her:
'Have done with sorrow;
I'll bring you plums tomorrow
Fresh on their mother twigs,
Cherries worth getting;
You cannot think what figs
My teeth have met in,

What melons icy-cold
Piled on a dish of gold
Too huge for me to hold,
What peaches with a velvet nap,
Pellucid grapes without one seed:
Odorous indeed must be the mead
Whereon they grow, and pure the wave they drink
With lilies at the brink,
And sugar-sweet their sap.'

Golden head by golden head,
Like two pigeons in one nest
Folded in each other's wings,
They lay down in their curtained bed:
Like two blossoms on one stem,
Like two flakes of new-fall'n snow,
Like two wands of ivory
Tipped with gold for awful kings.
Moon and stars gazed in at them,
Wind sang to them lullaby,
Lumbering owls forbore to fly,
Not a bat flapped to and fro
Round their rest:
Cheek to cheek and breast to breast
Locked together in one nest.

Early in the morning
When the first cock crowed his warning,
Neat like bees, as sweet and busy,
Laura rose with Lizzie:
Fetched in honey, milked the cows,
Aired and set to rights the house,
Kneaded cakes of whitest wheat,
Cakes for dainty mouths to eat,

Next churned butter, whipped up cream,
Fed their poultry, sat and sewed;
Talked as modest maidens should:
Lizzie with an open heart,
Laura in an absent dream,
One content, one sick in part;
One warbling for the mere bright day's delight,
One longing for the night.

At length slow evening came:
They went with pitchers to the reedy brook;
Lizzie most placid in her look,
Laura most like a leaping flame.
They drew the gurgling water from its deep.
Lizzie plucked purple and rich golden flags,
Then turning homeward said: 'The sunset flushes
Those furthest loftiest crags;
Come, Laura, not another maiden lags,
No wilful squirrel wags,
The beasts and birds are fast asleep.'
But Laura loitered still among the rushes
And said the bank was steep.

And said the hour was early still,
The dew not fall'n, the wind not chill;
Listening ever, but not catching
The customary cry,
'Come buy, come buy,'
With its iterated jingle
Of sugar-baited words:
Nor for all her watching
Once discerning even one goblin
Racing, whisking, tumbling, hobbling –

Let alone the herds
That used to tramp along the glen,
In groups or single,
Of brisk fruit-merchant men.

Till Lizzie urged, 'O Laura, come;
I hear the fruit-call, but I dare not look:
You should not loiter longer at this brook:
Come with me home.
The stars rise, the moon bends her arc,
Each glowworm winks her spark,
Let us get home before the night grows dark:
For clouds may gather
Though this is summer weather,
Put out the lights and drench us through;
Then if we lost our way what should we do?'

Laura turned cold as stone
To find her sister heard that cry alone,
That goblin cry,
'Come buy our fruits, come buy.'
Must she then buy no more such dainty fruit?
Must she no more such succous pasture find,
Gone deaf and blind?
Her tree of life drooped from the root:
She said not one word in her heart's sore ache:
But peering thro' the dimness, nought discerning,
Trudged home, her pitcher dripping all the way;
So crept to bed, and lay
Silent till Lizzie slept;
Then sat up in a passionate yearning.
And gnashed her teeth for baulked desire, and wept
As if her heart would break.

Day after day, night after night,
Laura kept watch in vain
In sullen silence of exceeding pain.
She never caught again the goblin cry,
'Come buy, come buy' –
She never spied the goblin men
Hawking their fruits along the glen:
But when the noon waxed bright
Her hair grew thin and grey;
She dwindled, as the fair full moon doth turn
To swift decay and burn
Her fire away.

One day remembering her kernel-stone
She set it by a wall that faced the south;
Dewed it with tears, hoped for a root,
Watched for a waxing shoot,
But there came none.
It never saw the sun,
It never felt the trickling moisture run:
While with sunk eyes and faded mouth
She dreamed of melons, as a traveller sees
False waves in desert drouth
With shade of leaf-crowned trees,
And burns the thirstier in the sandful breeze.

She no more swept the house,
Tended the fowls or cows,
Fetched honey, kneaded cakes of wheat,
Brought water from the brook:
But sat down listless in the chimney-nook
And would not eat.

Tender Lizzie could not bear
To watch her sister's cankerous care
Yet not to share.
She night and morning
Caught the goblins' cry:
'Come buy our orchard fruits,
Come buy, come buy' –
Beside the brook, along the glen,
She heard the tramp of goblin men,
The voice and stir
Poor Laura could not hear;
Longed to buy fruit to comfort her,
But feared to pay too dear.
She thought of Jeanie in her grave,
Who should have been a bride;
But who for joys brides hope to have
Fell sick and died
In her gay prime,
In earliest winter time,
With the first glazing rime,
With the first snow-fall of crisp winter time.
Till Laura dwindling
Seemed knocking at Death's door.
Then Lizzie weighed no more
Better and worse;
But put a silver penny in her purse,
Kissed Laura, crossed the heath with clumps of furze
At twilight, halted by the brook:
And for the first time in her life
Began to listen and look.

Laughed every goblin
When they spied her peeping:

Came towards her hobbling,
Flying, running, leaping,
Puffing and blowing,
Chuckling, clapping, crowing,
Clucking and gobbling,
Mopping and mowing,
Full of airs and graces,
· Pulling wry faces,
Demure grimaces,
Cat-like and rat-like,
Ratel- and wombat-like,
Snail-paced in a hurry,
Parrot-voiced and whistler,
Helter skelter, hurry skurry,
Chattering like magpies,
Fluttering like pigeons,
Gliding like fishes –
Hugged her and kissed her:
Squeezed and caressed her:
Stretched up their dishes,
Panniers, and plates:
'Look at our apples
Russet and dun,
Bob at our cherries,
Bite at our peaches,
Citrons and dates,
Grapes for the asking,
Pears red with basking
Out in the sun,
Plums on their twigs;
Pluck them and suck them,
Pomegranates, figs.'

'Good folk,' said Lizzie,
Mindful of Jeanie:
'Give me much and many:'
Held out her apron,
Tossed them her penny.
'Nay, take a seat with us,
Honour and eat with us,'
They answered grinning:
'Our feast is but beginning.
Night yet is early,
Warm and dew-pearly,
Wakeful and starry:
Such fruits as these
No man can carry;
Half their bloom would fly,
Half their dew would dry,
Half their flavour would pass by.
Sit down and feast with us,
Be welcome guest with us,
Cheer you and rest with us.' –
'Thank you,' said Lizzie: 'But one waits
At home alone for me:
So without further parleying,
If you will not sell me any
Of your fruits though much and many,
Give me back my silver penny
I tossed you for a fee.' –
They began to scratch their pates,
No longer wagging, purring,
But visibly demurring,
Grunting and snarling.
One called her proud,
Cross-grained, uncivil;
Their tones waxed loud,

Their looks were evil.
Lashing their tails
They trod and hustled her,
Elbowed and jostled her,
Clawed with their nails,
Barking, mewing, hissing, mocking,
Tore her gown and soiled her stocking,
Twitched her hair out by the roots,
Stamped upon her tender feet,
Held her hands and squeezed their fruits
Against her mouth to make her eat.

White and golden Lizzie stood,
Like a lily in a flood —
Like a rock of blue-veined stone
Lashed by tides obstreperously —
Like a beacon left alone
In a hoary roaring sea,
Sending up a golden fire —
Like a fruit-crowned orange-tree
White with blossoms honey-sweet
Sore beset by wasp and bee —
Like a royal virgin town
Topped with gilded dome and spire
Close beleaguered by a fleet
Mad to tug her standard down.

One may lead a horse to water,
Twenty cannot make him drink.
Though the goblins cuffed and caught her,
Coaxed and fought her,
Bullied and besought her,
Scratched her, pinched her black as ink,
Kicked and knocked her,

Mauled and mocked her,
Lizzie uttered not a word;
Would not open lip from lip
Lest they should cram a mouthful in:
But laughed in heart to feel the drip
Of juice that syruped all her face,
And lodged in dimples of her chin,
And streaked her neck which quaked like curd.
At last the evil people
Worn out by her resistance
Flung back her penny, kicked their fruit
Along whichever road they took,
Not leaving root or stone or shoot;
Some writhed into the ground,
Some dived into the brook
With ring and ripple,
Some scudded on the gale without a sound,
Some vanished in the distance.

In a smart, ache, tingle,
Lizzie went her way;
Knew not was it night or day;
Sprang up the bank, tore thro' the furze,
Threaded copse and dingle,
And heard her penny jingle
Bouncing in her purse –
Its bounce was music to her ear.
She ran and ran
As if she feared some goblin man
Dogged her with gibe or curse
Or something worse:
But not one goblin scurried after,
Nor was she pricked by fear;
The kind heart made her windy-paced

That urged her home quite out of breath with haste
And inward laughter.

She cried 'Laura,' up the garden,
'Did you miss me?
Come and kiss me.
Never mind my bruises,
Hug me, kiss me, suck my juices
Squeezed from goblin fruits for you,
Goblin pulp and goblin dew.
Eat me, drink me, love me;
Laura, make much of me;
For your sake I have braved the glen
And had to do with goblin merchant men.'

Laura started from her chair,
Flung her arms up in the air,
Clutched her hair:
'Lizzie, Lizzie, have you tasted
For my sake the fruit forbidden?
Must your light like mine be hidden,
Your young life like mine be wasted,
Undone in mine undoing
And ruined in my ruin,
Thirsty, cankered, goblin-ridden?' –
She clung about her sister,
Kissed and kissed and kissed her:
Tears once again
Refreshed her shrunken eyes,
Dropping like rain
After long sultry drouth;
Shaking with aguish fear, and pain,
She kissed and kissed her with a hungry mouth.

Her lips began to scorch,
That juice was wormwood to her tongue,
She loathed the feast:
Writing as one possessed she leaped and sung,
Rent all her robe, and wrung
Her hands in lamentable haste,
And beat her breast.
Her locks streamed like the torch
Borne by a racer at full speed,
Or like the mane of horses in their flight,
Or like an eagle when she stems the light
Straight toward the sun,
Or like a caged thing freed,
Or like a flying flag when armies run.

Swift fire spread through her veins, knocked at her heart,
Met the fire smouldering there
And overbore its lesser flame;
She gorged on bitterness without a name:
Ah fool, to choose such part
Of soul-consuming care!
Sense failed in the mortal strife:
Like the watch-tower of a town
Which an earthquake shatters down,
Like a lightning-stricken mast,
Like a wind-uprooted tree
Spun about,
Like a foam-topped waterspout
Cast down headlong in the sea,
She fell at last;
Pleasure past and anguish past,
Is it death or is it life?

Life out of death.
That night long Lizzie watched by her,
Counted her pulse's flagging stir,
Felt for her breath,
Held water to her lips and cooled her face
With tears and fanning leaves.
But when the first birds chirped about their eaves,
And early reapers plodded to the place
Of golden sheaves,
And dew-wet grass
Bowed in the morning winds to brisk to pass,
And new buds with new day
Opened of cup-like lilies on the stream,
Laura awoke as from a dream,
Laughed in the innocent old way,
Hugged Lizzie but not twice or thrice;
Her gleaming locks showed not one thread of grey,
Her breath was sweet as May,
And light danced in her eyes.

Days, weeks, months, years
Afterwards, when both were wives
With children of their own;
Their mother-hearts beset with fears,
Their lives bound up in tender lives;
Laura would call the little ones
And tell them of her early prime,
Those pleasant days long gone
Of not-returning time:
Would talk about the haunted glen,
The wicked, quaint fruit-merchant men,
Their fruits like honey to the throat
But poison in the blood;
(Men sell not such in any town):

Would tell them how her sister stood
In deadly peril to do her good,
And win the fiery antidote:
Then joining hands to little hands
Would bid them cling together –
'For there is no friend like a sister
In calm or stormy weather;
To cheer one on the tedious way,
To fetch one if one goes astray,
To lift one if one totters down,
To strengthen whilst one stands.'

CHRISTINA G. ROSSETTI

Dregs

The fire is out, and spent the warmth thereof,
(This is the end of every song man sings!)
The golden wine is drunk, the dregs remain,
Bitter as wormwood and as salt as pain;
And health and hope have gone the way of love
Into the drear oblivion of lost things.
Ghosts go along with us until the end;
This was a mistress, this, perhaps, a friend.
With pale, indifferent eyes, we sit and wait
For the dropt curtain and the closing gate:
This is the end of all the songs man sings.

ERNEST DOWSON

'Idle and light are many
things you see'

Idle and light are many things you see
In these my closing pages: blame not me.
However rich and plenteous the repast,
Nuts, almonds, biscuits, wafers come at last.

WALTER SAVAGE LANDOR
from *Interlude*

Author Notes

The ISBN given is that of the most recent Penguin edition.

ANONYMOUS (fl. *c.* 1624). 'A Songe bewailinge the tyme of Christmas, So much decayed in Englande' from *The Penguin Book of Renaissance Verse, 1509–1659* (0 14 042346 X).

SIR JOHN BEAUMONT (1583?–1627). 'He happy is, who farre from busie sounds' from *Horace in English* (0 14 042387 7).

ARNOLD BENNETT (1867–1931). 'The Misers' Wedding Breakfast' from *Riceyman Steps* (0 14 018259 4).

SIR JOHN BETJEMAN (1906–84). 'In a Bath Teashop' from *The Best of Betjeman* (0 14 018308 6).

SIR RICHARD BLACKMORE (1652–1729). 'The Digestive System' in *Eighteenth-Century English Verse* (0 14 042169 6).

WILLIAM BLAKE (1757–1827). 'I asked a thief to steal me a peach' from *English Romantic Verse* (0 14 042102 5) and *Complete Poems* (0 14 042215 3).

SAMUEL BUTLER (1835–1902). 'Turtle, Lobster and Punch' from *The Way of All Flesh* (0 14 043012 1).

LORD BYRON (1788–1824). 'The Sultan and the Dervise' from 'The Corsair' in *Selected Poems* (0 14 042381 8) and 'Lines Inscribed Upon a Cup Formed from a Skull' from *The Penguin Book of English Romantic Verse* (0 14 042102 5).

LEWIS CARROLL (1832–98). 'The Walrus and the Carpenter' and 'The Tea-Party' from *Alice's Adventures in Wonderland and Through the Looking Glass* (0 14 043317 1).

GEOFFREY CHAUCER (1342?–1400). All extracts from *The Canterbury Tales: The First Fragment* (o 14 043409 7).

WILLIAM COWPER (1731–1800). 'Boy, I hate their empty shows' from *Horace in English* (o 14 042387 7); 'To the Immortal Memory of the Halibut' and 'The Bee and the Pineapple' from *Selected Poems of Thomas Gray, Charles Churchill and William Cowper* (o 14 042401 6).

H.D. (HILDA DOOLITTLE) (1886–1961). 'Priapus' from *Imagist Poetry* (o 14 018368 X).

GEORGE DARLEY (1795–1846). 'Queen Eleanor and her Dwarf' from *English Romantic Verse* (o 14 042102 5).

CHARLES DICKENS (1812–70). 'At the Maypole' from *Barnaby Rudge* (o 14 043090 3); 'Scrooge Observes the Cratchit Christmas' from *A Christmas Carol* in *The Christmas Books Volume 1* (o 14 043068 7); 'The Kitchens at Epsom' from 'Epsom' in *Selected Journalism, 1850–1870* (o 14 043580 8); 'Smallweed, Jobling and Guppy at Dinner' from *Bleak House* (o 14 043496 8); 'Pie Fillings', 'The Magpie and Stump', 'The Marquis of Granby' and 'The Great White Horse' from *The Pickwick Papers* (o 14 043078 4).

JOHN DOS PASSOS (1896–1970). 'Eggs' and 'A Dinner in Manhattan' from *Manhattan Transfer* (o 14 008399 5).

ERNEST DOWSON (1867–1900). 'Dregs' from *Poetry of the 1890s* (o 14 043639 1).

MICHAEL DRAYTON (1563–1631). 'That *Phœbus* in his lofty race' from 'The Muses of Elysium' in *The Penguin Book of Renaissance Verse, 1509–1659* (o 14 042346 X).

JOHN DRYDEN (1631–1700). 'How happy in his low degree' from *Horace in English* (o 14 042387 7).

JAMES ELPHINSTON (1721–1809). 'To Ligurinus' from *Martial in English* (0 14 042389 3).

EDWARD FITZGERALD (1809–93). 'And lately, by the Tavern Door agape' from *The Rubáiyát of Omar Khayyám* in *The Penguin Book of Victorian Verse* (0 14 044578 1).

F. SCOTT FITZGERALD (1896–1940). 'Gatsby's Parties' from *The Great Gatsby* (0 14 018067 2).

FORD MADOX FORD (1873–1939). 'Mrs Duchemin's Breakfast' from *Some Do Not . . .* in *Parade's End* (0 14 018083 4).

E. M. FORSTER (1879–1970). 'A Dinner in Italy' from *Where Angels Fear to Tread* (0 14 018088 5).

THOMAS GRAY (1716–71). 'Ode on the Death of a Favourite Cat' from *Selected Poems of Thomas Gray, Charles Churchill and William Cowper* (0 14 042401 6).

PATRICK HAMILTON (1904–62). 'The Night Before the Morning After' from *Hangover Square* (0 14 018397 3).

SIR JOHN HARINGTON (*c.* 1560–1612). 'To One that had Meate Ill Drest' from *Martial in English* (0 14 042389 3).

WILLIAM HAY (1695–1755). 'You sweep my table: sausages, and chine' and 'In leathern jack to drink much less I hate' from *Martial in English* (0 14 042389 3).

JAMES HENRY (1798–1876). 'The húman skull is of deceit' from *The Penguin Book of Victorian Verse* (0 14 044578 1).

GEORGE HERBERT (1593–1633). 'Love (3)' from *The Complete English Poems* (0 14 042348 6).

ROBERT HERRICK (1591–1674). 'The Custard' from *Martial in English* (0 14 042389 3) and 'The Wassaile' from *The Penguin Book of Renaissance Verse, 1509–1659* (0 14 042346 X).

GERARD MANLEY HOPKINS (1844–89). 'Ah child, no Persian – perfect art!' from *Horace in English* (0 14 042387 7).

HENRY JAMES (1843–1916). '*Omelette aux tomates*' from *The Ambassadors* (0 14 043233 7).

BEN JONSON (1572–1637). 'Inuiting a Friend to Supper' from *Martial in English* (0 14 042389 3) and *The Penguin Book of Renaissance Verse* (0 14 042346 X); 'Happie is he, that from all Businesse cleere' from *Horace in English* (0 14 042387 7).

JOHN KEATS (1795–1821). 'To Autumn' from *The Complete Poems* (0 14 042210 2).

CHARLES KINGSLEY (1819–75). 'The Poetry of a Root Crop' from *The Penguin Book of Victorian Verse* (0 14 044578 1).

WALTER SAVAGE LANDOR (1775–1864). 'Idle and light are many things you see' from *Interlude* in *Martial in English* (0 14 042389 3).

EDWARD LEAR (1812–88). 'The Owl and the Pussy-Cat' from *The Penguin Book of Victorian Verse* (0 14 044578 1).

WYNDHAM LEWIS (1882–1957). 'The Restaurant Vallet' from *Tarr* (o/p 0 14 018264 0).

ANDREW MARVELL (1621–78). 'He lands us on a grassy stage' extracted from 'Bermudas' in *The Complete Poems* (0 14 042213 7).

HENRY MAYHEW (1812–87). 'Of the Street-Sellers of Cakes, Tarts, &c.' from *London Labour and the London Poor* (0 14 043241 8).

HERMAN MELVILLE (1819–91). 'First Breakfast at Sea' from *Redburn* (0 14 043105 5) and 'Herba Santa' from *Nineteenth-Century American Poetry* (0 14 043587 5).

JOHN MILTON (1608–74). 'Eden' and 'The Tempter and Eve' from *Paradise Lost* and 'Desire of wine and all delicious drinks' from *Samson Agonistes* in *The Complete Poems* (0 14 043363 5).

LADY MARY WORTLEY MONTAGU (1689–1762). All extracts from *Selected Letters* (0 14 043490 9).

THOMAS NASHE (1567–*c*. 1600). 'Gluttony and Drunkenness' from *Pierce Penniless* in *The Unfortunate Traveller and Other Works* (0 14 043067 9).

GEORGE ORWELL (1903–50). 'Back in Lower Binfield' from *Coming Up for Air* (0 14 018228 4) and 'Hunger and Poverty' from *Down and Out in Paris and London* (0 14 018230 6).

'DR P.' (possibly WALTER POPE d. 1714). 'What? Quarrel in your drink, my friends?' from *Horace in English* (0 14 042387 7).

THOMAS LOVE PEACOCK (1785–1866). 'Christmas at Chainmail Hall' from *Crotchet Castle* in *Nightmare Abbey/Crotchet Castle* (0 14 043045 8) and 'Seamen Three' from *English Romantic Verse* (0 14 042102 5).

ALEXANDER POPE (1688–1744). 'The Tale of the Two Mice' from *Horace in English* (0 14 042387 7).

CHRISTINA G. ROSSETTI (1830–94). 'What does the bee do?' and *Goblin Market* from *The Penguin Book of Victorian Verse* (0 14 044578 1).

SAKI (H. H. MUNRO) (1870–1916). 'The Byzantine Omelette' from *Beasts and Super-Beasts* in *The Complete Saki* (0 14 018420 1).

SIR WALTER SCOTT (1771–1832). 'The Laird's Hospitality' from *The Tale of Old Mortality* (0 14 043653 7).

SIR CHARLES SEDLEY (1639–1701). 'To Classicus' from *Martial in English* (0 14 042389 3).

RICHARD BRINSLEY SHERIDAN (1751–1816). 'Song' from *The School for Scandal* in *The School for Scandal and Other Plays* (0 14 043240 X).

CHRISTOPHER SMART (1722–71). Extracts from 'A Song to David' in both Smart's *Selected Poems* (0 14 042367 2) and *The Psalms in English* (0 14 044618 4).

GOLDWIN SMITH (1823–1910). 'Faustinus is a man of taste' from *Martial in English* (0 14 042389 3).

TOBIAS SMOLLETT (1721–71). 'Country and Town' from *Humphry Clinker* (0 14 043021 0).

EDMUND SPENSER (1552?–99). 'Now al is done; bring home the bride againe' from *Epithalamion* in *The Penguin Book of Renaissance Verse, 1509–1659* (0 14 042346 X).

LAURENCE STERNE (1713–68). 'The *Pâtés* Seller' and 'A Peasant Supper' from *A Sentimental Journey* (0 14 043026 1).

ROBERT LOUIS STEVENSON (1850–94). 'On Attwater's Atoll' from *The Ebb-Tide* in *Dr Jekyll and Mr Hyde and Other Stories* (0 14 043117 9).

BRAM STOKER (1847–1912). 'Dinner at Castle Dracula' and 'Flies, Spiders and a Sparrow' from *Dracula* (0 14 043381 3).

JONATHAN SWIFT (1667–1745). All prose extracts from *Gulliver's Travels* (0 14 043022 9); 'Green Leeks' from *Martial in English* (0 14 042389 3).

ARTHUR SYMONS (1865–1945). 'At the Cavour' from *Poetry of the 1890s* (0 14 043639 1) and 'The Absinthe Drinker' from *The Penguin Book of Victorian Verse* (0 14 044578 1).

JULIAN SYMONS (1912–94). 'Pub' from *Poetry of the Forties* (0 14 018369 8).

SIR JOHN TENNIEL (1820–1914). Two illustrations from *Alice's Adventures in Wonderland and Through the Looking Glass* (0 14 043317 1).

WILLIAM MAKEPEACE THACKERAY (1811–63). 'The Bowl of Rack Punch' from *Vanity Fair* (0 14 043035 0) and 'The Three Sailors' from *The Penguin Book of Victorian Verse* (0 14 044578 1).

FLORA THOMPSON (1876–1947). 'At the *Wagon and Horses*' from *Lark Rise* and 'Journeyman Meals' from *Over to Candleford*, both in *Lark Rise to Candleford* (0 14 018850 9).

HENRY DAVID THOREAU (1817–62). 'Appetite' and 'Flesh and Fat' from *Walden* in *Walden and Civil Disobedience* (0 14 039044 8).

HENRY VAUGHAN (*c.* 1621–95). 'But if to ease his busy breast' from 'Translation of Casimir' in *The Complete Poems* (0 14 042208 0).

EVELYN WAUGH (1903–66). 'On the Guyana–Brazil Border' from *Ninety-Two Days* (0 14 018840 1) and 'School during Wartime' from *A Little Learning* (0 14 018309 4).

AUGUSTA WEBSTER (1837–94). Extract from 'Circe' from *Victorian Verse* (o/p 0 14 042110 6).

JOHN GREENLEAF WHITTIER (1807–92). 'The Haschish' from *Nineteenth-Century American Poetry* (0 14 043587 5).

VIRGINIA WOOLF (1882–1941). '*Boeuf en Daube*' from *To the Lighthouse* (0 14 018572 0).

Acknowledgements

The publishers gratefully acknowledge the following for permission to reprint copyright poems and prose extracts in this volume:

ARNOLD BENNETT: 'The Miser's Wedding Breakfast' from *Riceyman Steps* (Penguin Twentieth-Century Classics, 1991), to A. P. Watt Ltd on behalf of Mme V. M. Eldin; JOHN BETJEMAN: 'In a Bath Teashop' from *Collected Poems*, to John Murray (Publishers) Ltd. (Reprinted by Penguin in *The Best of Betjeman*, edited by John Guest); H. D. (HILDA DOOLITTLE: 'Orchard' from *Collected Poems 1912–1944* (Carcanet, 1984) to Carcanet Press and New Directions Publishing Corporation. (This poem is reprinted by Penguin under the title of 'Priapus' in *Imagist Poetry*, edited by Peter Jones); JOHN DOS PASSOS: 'Eggs' and 'A Dinner in Manhattan' from *Manhattan Transfer* (Penguin Twentieth-Century Classics, 1989), copyright © John Dos Passos, 1925, to The Estate of the Late John Dos Passos and A. M. Heath & Company Ltd; F. SCOTT FITZGERALD: 'Gatsby's Parties' from *The Great Gatsby* (Penguin Twentieth-Century Classics, 1990), to David Higham Associates Ltd; FORD MADOX FORD: 'Mrs Duchemin's Breakfast' from *Some Do Not . . .* in *Parade's End* (Penguin Books, 1990), to David Higham Associates Ltd; E. M. FORSTER: 'A Dinner in Italy' from *Where Angels Fear to Tread* (Penguin Twentieth-Century Classics, 1989), copyright 1920 by Alfred A. Knopf Inc. and renewed 1948 by Edward Morgan Forster, to The Provost and Scholars of King's College, Cambridge, and The Society of Authors as the literary representatives of the E. M. Forster Estate, and Alfred A. Knopf Inc.; PATRICK HAMILTON: 'The Night Before the Morning

After' from *Hangover Square* (Constable, 1972; Penguin Twentieth-Century Classics, 1990), to Constable & Co. Ltd; GERARD MANLEY HOPKINS: Ode 1.38, 'Ah child, no Persian – perfect art!' from *Horace in English*, edited by D. S. Carne-Ross and Kenneth Haynes (Penguin Classics, 1996), originally published in *The Poetical Works of Gerard Manley Hopkins*, edited by Norman H. MacKenzie (1980), to Oxford University Press on behalf of the Society of Jesus; WYNDHAM LEWIS: 'The Restaurant Vallet' from *Tarr* (Penguin Twentieth-Century Classics, 1989), © Wyndham Lewis and the estate of the late Mrs G. A. Wyndham Lewis by kind permission of the Wyndham Lewis Memorial Trust (a registered charity); GEORGE ORWELL: 'Back in Lower Binstead' from *Coming Up for Air* (Penguin Twentieth-Century Classics, 1990), copyright © George Orwell, 1939, and 'Hunger and Poverty' from *Down and Out in Paris and London* (Penguin Books, 1989), copyright © George Orwell, 1933, to Mark Hamilton as the Literary Executor of the Estate of the Late Sonia Brownell Orwell and Martin Secker & Warburg Ltd; ARTHUR SYMONS: 'At the Cavour' from *Poetry of the 1890s*, edited by R. K. R. Thornton and Marion Thain (Penguin Classics, 1997), and 'The Absinthe Drinker' from the *Penguin Book of Victorian Verse*, edited by Daniel Karlin (Allen Lane/The Penguin Press, 1997), both originally published in *Silhouettes* (2nd edition 1896), to Mr Brian Read, M. A. (Oxon); JULIAN SYMONS: 'Pub' from *Poetry of the Forties*, edited by Robin Skelton (Penguin Twentieth-Century Classics, 1990), to Curtis Brown Ltd on behalf of the Estate of Julian Symons; FLORA THOMPSON: 'At the Wagon and Horses' and 'Journeyman Meals' from *Lark Rise to Candleford* (Oxford University Press, 1945; Penguin Books, 1989), to Oxford University Press; EVELYN WAUGH: 'On the Guyana-Brazil Border' from *Ninety-Two Days* (Metheun, 1991) and 'School during Wartime' from *A Little Learning* (Penguin Twentieth-Century Classics, 1990), to The Peters Fraser & Dunlop Group Ltd; VIRGINIA WOOLF: 'Boeuf en Daube' from

To the Lighthouse (Penguin Twentieth-Century Classics, 1992), to The Society of Authors as the Literary Representative of the Estate of Virginia Woolf.